LEGION and THE EMPEROR'S SOUL

BRANDON SANDERSON

First published in Great Britain in 2013 by
Gollancz
An imprint of the Orion Publishing Group
Orion House, 5 Upper St Martin's Lane,
London WC2H 9EA
An Hachette UK Company

This edition published in Great Britain
in 2014 by Gollancz

1 3 5 7 9 10 8 6 4 2

A CIP catalogue record for this book is available
from the British Library

ISBN 978 0 575 11634 4

Typeset by Input Data Services Ltd, Bridgwater, Somerset

Printed in Great Britain by Clays Ltd, St Ives plc

The Orion Publishing Group's policy is to use papers that are natural, renewable and recyclable products and made from wood grown in sustainable forests. The logging and manufacturing processes are expected to conform to the environmental regulations of the country of origin.

www.brandonsanderson.com
www.orionbooks.co.uk
www.gollancz.co.uk

CONTENTS

LEGION

For Daniel Wells, who gave me the idea.

My name is Stephen Leeds, and I am perfectly sane. My hallucinations, however, are all quite mad.

The gunshots coming from J.C.'s room popped like firecrackers. Grumbling to myself, I grabbed the earmuffs hanging outside his door – I'd learned to keep them there – and pushed my way in. J.C. wore his own earmuffs, his handgun raised in two hands, sighting at a picture of Osama bin Laden on the wall.

Beethoven was playing. Very loudly.

'I was trying to have a conversation!' I yelled.

J.C. didn't hear me. He emptied a clip into bin Laden's face, punching an assortment of holes through the wall in the process. I didn't dare get close. He might accidentally shoot me if I surprised him.

I didn't know what would happen if one of my hallucinations shot me. How would my mind interpret that? Undoubtedly, there were a dozen psychologists who'd want to write a paper on it. I wasn't inclined to give them the opportunity.

'J.C.!' I screamed as he stopped to reload.

He glanced toward me, then grinned, taking off his earmuffs. Any grin from J.C. looks half like a scowl, but I'd long ago learned to stop being intimidated by him.

'Eh, skinny,' he said, holding up the handgun. 'Care to fire off a clip or two? You could use the practice.'

I took the gun from him. 'We had a shooting range installed in the mansion for a purpose, J.C. *Use it.*'

'Terrorists don't usually find me in a shooting range. Well, it did happen that once. Pure coincidence.'

I sighed, taking the remote from the end table, then turning down the music. J.C. reached out, pointing the tip of the gun up in the air, then moving my finger off the trigger. 'Safety first, kid.'

'It's an imaginary gun anyway,' I said, handing it back to him.

'Yeah, sure.'

J.C. doesn't believe that he's a hallucination, which is unusual. Most of them accept it, to one extent or another. Not J.C. Big without being bulky, square-faced but not distinctive, he had the eyes of a killer. Or so he claimed. Perhaps he kept them in his pocket.

He slapped a new clip into the gun, then eyed the picture of bin Laden.

'Don't,' I warned.

'But—'

'He's dead anyway. They got him ages ago.'

'That's a story we told the public, skinny.' J.C. holstered the gun. 'I'd explain, but you don't have clearance.'

'Stephen?' a voice came from the doorway.

I turned. Tobias is another hallucination – or 'aspect,' as I sometimes call them. Lanky and ebony-skinned, he had dark freckles on his age-wrinkled cheeks. He kept his greying hair very short, and wore a loose, informal business suit with no necktie.

'I was merely wondering,' Tobias said, 'how long you intend to keep that poor man waiting.'

'Until he leaves,' I said, joining Tobias in the hallway. The two of us began walking away from J.C.'s room.

'He was very polite, Stephen,' Tobias said.

Behind us, J.C. started shooting again. I groaned.

'I'll go speak to J.C.,' Tobias said in a soothing voice. 'He's just trying to keep up his skills. He wants to be of use to you.'

'Fine, whatever.' I left Tobias and rounded a corner in the lush mansion. I had forty-seven rooms. They were nearly all filled. At the end of the hallway, I entered a small room decorated with a Persian rug and wood panels. I threw myself down on the black leather couch in the center.

Ivy sat at her chair beside the couch. 'You intend to continue through *that*?' she asked over the sound of the gunshots.

'Tobias is going to speak to him.'

'I see,' Ivy said, making a notation on her notepad. She wore a dark business suit, with slacks and a jacket. Her blonde hair was up in a bun. She was in her early forties, and was one of the aspects I'd had the longest.

'How does it make you feel,' she said, 'that your projections are beginning to disobey you?'

'Most do obey me,' I said defensively. 'J.C. has *never* paid attention to what I tell him. That hasn't changed.'

'You deny that it's getting worse?'

I didn't say anything.

She made a notation.

'You turned away another petitioner, didn't you?' Ivy asked. 'They come to you for help.'

'I'm busy.'

'Doing what? Listening to gunshots? Going more mad?'

'I'm *not* going more mad,' I said. 'I've stabilized. I'm practically normal. Even my non-hallucinatory psychiatrist acknowledges that.'

Ivy said nothing. In the distance, the gunshots finally stopped, and I sighed in relief, raising my fingers to my temples. 'The formal definition of insanity,' I said, 'is actually quite fluid. Two people can have the exact same condition, with the exact same severity, but one can be considered *sane* by the official standards while the other is considered *insane*. You cross the line into insanity when your mental state stops you from being able to function, from being able to have a normal life. By those standards, I'm not the least bit insane.'

'You call this a normal life?' she asked.

'It works well enough.' I glanced to the side. Ivy had covered up the wastebasket with a clipboard, as usual.

Tobias entered a few moments later. 'That petitioner is still there, Stephen.'

'What?' Ivy said, giving me a glare. 'You're making the poor man wait? It's been *four hours*.'

'All right, fine!' I leaped off the couch. 'I'll send him away.' I strode out of the room and down the steps to the ground floor, into the grand entryway.

Wilson, my butler – who is a real person, not a hallucination – stood outside the closed door to the sitting room. He looked over his bifocals at me.

'You too?' I asked.

'Four hours, master?'

'I had to get myself under control, Wilson.'

'You like to use that excuse, Master Leeds. One wonders if moments like this are a matter of laziness more than control.'

'You're not paid to wonder things like that,' I said.

He raised an eyebrow, and I felt ashamed. Wilson didn't deserve snappishness; he was an excellent servant, and an excellent person. It wasn't easy to find house staff willing to put up with my ... particularities.

'I'm sorry,' I said. 'I've been feeling a little worn down lately.'

'I will fetch you some lemonade, Master Leeds,' he said. 'For ...'

'Three of us,' I said, nodding to Tobias and Ivy – who, of course, Wilson couldn't see. 'Plus the petitioner.'

'No ice in mine, please,' Tobias said.

'I'll have a glass of water instead,' Ivy added.

'No ice for Tobias,' I said, absently pushing open the door. 'Water for Ivy.'

Wilson nodded, off to do as requested. He *was* a good butler. Without him, I think I'd go insane.

A young man in a polo shirt and slacks waited in the sitting room. He leaped up from one of the chairs. 'Master Legion?'

I winced at the nickname. That had been chosen by a particularly gifted psychologist. Gifted in dramatics, that is. Not really so much in the psychology department.

'Call me Stephen,' I said, holding the door for Ivy and Tobias. 'What can we do for you?'

'We?' the boy asked.

'Figure of speech,' I said, walking into the room and taking one of the chairs across from the young man.

'I ... uh ... I hear you help people, when nobody else will.' The boy swallowed. 'I brought two thousand. Cash.' He tossed an envelope with my name and address on it onto the table.

'That'll buy you a consultation,' I said, opening it and doing a quick count.

Tobias gave me a look. He hates it when I charge people,

but you don't get a mansion with enough rooms to hold all your hallucinations by working for free. Besides, judging from his clothing, this kid could afford it.

'What's the problem?' I asked.

'My fiancée,' the young man said, taking something out of his pocket. 'She's been cheating on me.'

'My condolences,' I said. 'But we're *not* private investigators. We don't do surveillance.'

Ivy walked through the room, not sitting down. She strolled around the young man's chair, inspecting him.

'I know,' the boy said quickly. 'I just . . . well, she's vanished, you see.'

Tobias perked up. He likes a good mystery.

'He's not telling us everything,' Ivy said, arms folded, one finger tapping her other arm.

'You sure?' I asked.

'Oh, yes,' the boy said, assuming I'd spoken to him. 'She's gone, though she did leave this note.' He unfolded it and set it on the table. 'The really strange thing is, I think there might be some kind of cipher to it. Look at these words. They don't make sense.'

I picked up the paper, scanning the words he indicated. They were on the back of the sheet, scrawled quickly, like a list of notes. The same paper had later been used as a farewell letter from the fiancée. I showed it to Tobias.

'That's Plato,' he said, pointing to the notes on the back. 'Each is a quote from the *Phaedrus*. Ah, Plato. Remarkable man, you know. Few people are aware that he was actually a *slave* at one point, sold on the market by a tyrant who disagreed with his politics – that and the turning of the tyrant's brother into a disciple. Fortunately, Plato was purchased by someone familiar with his work, an admirer you might say, who freed him. It does pay to have loving fans, even in ancient Greece …'

Tobias continued on. He had a deep, comforting voice, which I liked to listen to. I examined the note, then looked up at Ivy, who shrugged.

The door opened, and Wilson entered with the lemonade and Ivy's water. I noticed J.C. standing outside, his gun out as he peeked into the room and inspected the young man. J.C.'s eyes narrowed.

'Wilson,' I said, taking my lemonade, 'would you kindly send for Audrey?'

'Certainly, master,' the butler said. I knew, somewhere deep within, that he had not *really* brought cups for Ivy and Tobias, though he made an act of handing something to the empty chairs. My mind filled in the rest, imagining drinks, imagining Ivy strolling over to pluck hers from Wilson's hand as he tried to give it to where he thought she was sitting. She smiled at him fondly.

Wilson left.

'Well?' the young man asked. 'Can you—'

He cut off as I held up a finger. Wilson couldn't see my projections, but he knew their rooms. We had to hope that Audrey was in. She had a habit of visiting her sister in Springfield.

Fortunately, she walked into the room a few minutes later. She was, however, wearing a bathrobe. 'I assume this is important,' she said, drying her hair with a towel.

I held up the note, then the envelope with the money. Audrey leaned down. She was a dark-haired woman, a little on the chunky side. She'd joined us a few years back, when I'd been working on a counterfeiting case.

She mumbled to herself for a minute or two, taking out a magnifying glass – I was amused that she kept one in her bathrobe, but that was Audrey for you – and looking from the note to the envelope and back. One had supposedly been written by the fiancée, the other by the young man.

Audrey nodded. 'Definitely the same hand.'

'It's not a very big sample,' I said.

'It's what?' the boy asked.

'It's enough in this case,' Audrey said. 'The envelope has your full name and address. Line slant, word spacing, letter formation … all give the same answer. He also has a very distinctive *e*. If we use the longer sample as the exemplar, the envelope sample can be determined as authentic – in my estimation – at over a ninety percent reliability.'

'Thanks,' I said.

'I could use a new dog,' she said, strolling away.

'I'm *not* imagining you a puppy, Audrey. J.C. creates enough racket! I don't want a dog running around here barking.'

'Oh, come on,' she said, turning at the doorway. 'I'll feed it fake food and give it fake water and take it on fake walks. Everything a fake puppy could want.'

'Out with you,' I said, though I was smiling. She was teasing. It was nice to have some aspects who didn't mind being hallucinations. The young man regarded me with a baffled expression.

'You can drop the act,' I said to him.

'Act?'

'The act that you're surprised by how "strange" I am. This was a fairly amateur attempt. You're a grad student, I assume?'

He got a panicked look in his eyes.

'Next time, have a roommate write the note for you,' I said, tossing it back to him. 'Damn it, I don't have time for this.' I stood up.

'You could give him an interview,' Tobias said.

'After he lied to me?' I snapped.

'Please,' the boy said, standing. 'My girlfriend ...'

'You called her a fiancée before,' I said, turning. 'You're here to try to get me to take on a "case," during which you will lead me around by the nose while you secretly take notes about my condition. Your real purpose is to write a dissertation or something.'

His face fell. Ivy stood behind him, shaking her head in disdain.

'You think you're the first one to think of this?' I asked.

He grimaced. 'You can't blame a guy for trying.'

'I can and I do,' I said. 'Often. Wilson! We're going to need security!'

'No need,' the boy said, grabbing his things. In his haste, a miniature recorder slipped out of his shirt pocket and rattled against the table.

I raised an eyebrow as he blushed, snatched the recorder, then dashed from the room.

Tobias rose and walked over to me, his hands clasped behind his back. 'Poor lad. And he'll probably have to walk home, too. In the rain.'

'It's raining?'

'Stan says it will come soon,' Tobias said. 'Have you considered that they would try things like this less often if you would agree to an interview now and then?'

'I'm tired of being referenced in case studies,' I said, waving a hand in annoyance. 'I'm tired of being poked and prodded. I'm tired of being special.'

'What?' Ivy said, amused. 'You'd rather work a day job at a desk? Give up the spacious mansion?'

'I'm not saying there aren't perks,' I said as Wilson walked back in, turning his head to watch the youth flee out the front door. 'Make sure he actually goes, would you please, Wilson?'

'Of course, master.' He handed me a tray with the day's mail on it, then left.

I looked through the mail. He'd already removed the bills and the junk mail. That left a letter from my human psychologist, which I ignored, and a nondescript white envelope, large sized.

I frowned, taking it and ripping open the top. I took out the contents.

There was only one thing in the envelope. A single photograph, five by eight, in black and white. I raised an eyebrow. It was a picture of a rocky coast where a couple of small trees clung to a rock extending out into the ocean.

'Nothing on the back,' I said as Tobias and Ivy looked over my shoulder. 'Nothing else in the envelope.'

'It's from someone else trying to fish for an interview, I'll bet,' Ivy said. 'They're doing a better job than the kid.'

'It doesn't look like anything special,' J.C. said, shoving his way up beside Ivy, who punched him in the shoulder. 'Rocks. Trees. Boring.'

'I don't know . . .' I said. 'There's something about it. Tobias?'

Tobias took the photograph. At least, that's what I saw. Most likely I still had the photo in my hand, but I couldn't feel it there, now that I perceived Tobias holding it. It's strange, the way the mind can change perception.

Tobias studied the picture for a long moment. J.C. began clicking his pistol's safety off and on.

'Aren't you always talking about gun safety?' Ivy hissed at him.

'I'm being safe,' he said. 'Barrel's not pointed at anyone. Besides, I have keen, iron control over every muscle in my body. I could—'

'Hush, both of you,' Tobias said. He held the picture closer. 'My God . . .'

'Please don't use the Lord's name in vain,' Ivy said.

J.C. snorted.

'Stephen,' Tobias said. 'Computer.'

I joined him at the sitting room's desktop, then sat down, Tobias leaning over my shoulder. 'Do a search for the Lone Cypress.'

I did so, and brought up image view. A couple dozen shots of the same rock appeared on the screen, but all of them had a larger tree growing on it. The tree in these photos was fully grown; in fact, it looked ancient.

'Okay, great,' J.C. said. 'Still trees. Still rocks. Still boring.'

'That's the Lone Cypress, J.C.,' Tobias said. 'It's famous, and is believed to be *at least* two hundred and fifty years old.'

'So . . . ?' Ivy asked.

I held up the photograph that had been mailed. 'In this, it's no more than . . . what? Ten?'

'Likely younger,' Tobias said.

'So for this to be real,' I said, 'it would have to have been taken in the mid to late 1700s. Decades before the camera was invented.'

'LOOK, IT'S OBVIOUSLY a fake,' Ivy said. 'I don't see why you two are so bothered by this.'

Tobias and I strolled the hallway of the mansion. It had been two days. I still couldn't get the image out of my head. I carried the photo in my jacket pocket.

'A hoax *would* be the most rational explanation, Stephen,' Tobias said.

'Armando thinks it's real,' I said.

'Armando is a complete loon,' Ivy replied. Today she wore a grey business suit.

'True,' I said, then raised a hand to my pocket again. Altering the photo wouldn't have taken much. What was doctoring a photo, these days? Practically any kid with Photoshop could create realistic fakes.

Armando had run it through some advanced programs, checking levels and doing a bunch of other things that were too technical for me to understand, but he admitted that didn't mean anything. A talented artist could fool the tests.

So why did this photo haunt me so?

'This smacks of someone trying to prove something,' I said. 'There are many trees older than the Lone Cypress, but few are in as distinctive a location. This photograph is intended to be instantly recognizable as impossible, at least to those with a good knowledge of history.'

'All the more likely a hoax then, wouldn't you say?' Ivy asked.

'Perhaps.'

I paced back the other direction, my aspects growing silent. Finally, I heard the door shut below. I hurried to the landing down.

'Master?' Wilson said, climbing the steps.

'Wilson! Mail has arrived?'

He stopped at the landing, holding a silver tray. Megan, of

the cleaning staff – real, of course – scurried up behind him and passed us, face down, steps quick.

'She'll quit soon,' Ivy noted. 'You really should try to be less strange.'

'Tall order, Ivy,' I mumbled, looking through the mail. 'With you people around.' There! Another envelope, identical to the first. I tore into it eagerly and pulled out another picture.

This one was more blurry. It was of a man standing at a washbasin, towel at his neck. His surroundings were old-fashioned. It was also in black and white.

I turned the picture to Tobias. He took it, holding it up, inspecting it with eyes lined at the corners.

'Well?' Ivy asked.

'He looks familiar,' I said. 'I feel I should know him.'

'George Washington,' Tobias said. 'Having a morning shave, it appears. I'm surprised he didn't have someone to do it for him.'

'He was a soldier,' I said, taking the photo back. 'He was probably accustomed to doing things for himself.' I ran my fingers over the glossy picture. The first daguerreotype – early photographs – had been taken in the mid-1830s. Before that, nobody had been able to create permanent images of this nature. Washington had died in 1799.

'Look, this one is *obviously* a fake,' Ivy said. 'A picture of George Washington? We're to assume that someone went back in time, and the only thing they could think to do was grab a candid of George in the bathroom? We're being played, Steve.'

'Maybe,' I admitted.

'It does look *remarkably* like him,' Tobias said.

'Except we don't have any photos of him,' Ivy said. 'So there's no way to prove it. Look, all someone would have to do is hire a look-alike actor, pose the photo, and *bam*. They wouldn't even have to do any photo editing.'

'Let's see what Armando thinks,' I said, turning over the photo. On the back of this one was a phone number. 'Someone fetch Audrey first .'

'YOU MAY APPROACH His Majesty,' Armando said. He stood at his window, which was triangular – he occupied one of the peaks of the mansion. He'd demanded the position.

'Can I shoot him?' J.C. asked me softly. 'You know, in a place that's not important? A foot, maybe?'

'His Majesty heard that,' Armando said in his soft Spanish accent, turning unamused eyes our direction. 'Stephen Leeds. Have you fulfilled your promise to me? I must be restored to my throne.'

'Working on it, Armando,' I said, handing him the picture. 'We've got another one.'

Armando sighed, taking the photo from my fingers. He was a thin man with black hair he kept slicked back. 'Armando *benevolently* agrees to consider your supplication.' He held it up.

'You know, Steve,' Ivy said, poking through the room, 'if you're going to create hallucinations, you really should consider making them less annoying.'

'Silence, woman,' Armando said. 'Have you considered His Majesty's request?'

'I'm not going to marry you, Armando.'

'You would be queen!'

'You don't have a throne. And last I checked, Mexico has a president, not an emperor.'

'Drug lords threaten my people,' Armando said, inspecting the picture. 'They starve, and are forced to bow to the whims of foreign powers. It is a disgrace. This picture, it is authentic.' He handed it back.

'That's all?' I asked. 'You don't need to do some of those computer tests?'

'Am I not the photography expert?' Armando said. 'Did you not come to me with piteous supplication? I have spoken. It is real. No trickery. The photographer, however, is a buffoon. He knows nothing of the *art* of the craft. These pictures offend me in their utter pedestrian nature.' He turned his back to us, looking out the window again.

'*Now* can I shoot him?' J.C. asked.

'I'm tempted to let you,' I said, turning over the picture. Audrey had looked at the handwriting on the back, and hadn't been able to trace it to any of the professors, psychologists, or other groups that kept wanting to do studies on me.

I shrugged, then took out my phone. The number was local. It rang once before being picked up.

'Hello?' I said.

'May I come visit you, Mister Leeds?' A woman's voice, with a faint Southern accent.

'Who are you?'

'The person who has been sending you puzzles.'

'Well, I figured *that* part out.'

'May I come visit?'

'I . . . well, I suppose. Where are you?'

'Outside your gates.' The phone clicked. A moment later, chimes rang as someone buzzed the front gates.

I looked at the others. J.C. pushed his way to the window, gun out, and peeked at the front driveway. Armando scowled at him.

Ivy and I walked out of Armando's rooms toward the steps.

'You armed?' J.C. asked, jogging up to us.

'Normal people don't walk around their own homes with a gun strapped on, J.C.'

'They do if they want to live. Go get your gun.'

I hesitated, then sighed. 'Let her in, Wilson!' I called, but redirected to my own rooms – the largest in the complex – and took my handgun out of my nightstand. I holstered it under my arm and put my jacket back on. It did feel good to be armed, but I'm a *horrible* shot.

By the time I was making my way down the steps to the front entryway, Wilson had answered the door. A dark-skinned woman in her thirties stood at the doorway, wearing a black jacket, a business suit, and short dreadlocks. She took off her sunglasses and nodded to me.

'The sitting room, Wilson,' I said, reaching the landing. He led her to it, and I entered after, waiting for J.C. and Ivy to pass. Tobias already sat inside, reading a history book.

'Lemonade?' Wilson asked.

'No, thank you,' I said, pulling the door closed, Wilson outside.

The woman strolled around the room, looking over the décor. 'Fancy place,' she said. 'You paid for all of this with money from people who ask you for help?'

'Most of it came from the government,' I said.

'Word on the street says you don't work for them.'

'I don't, but I used to. Anyway, a lot of this came from

grant money. Professors who wanted to research me. I started charging enormous sums for the privilege, assuming it would put them off.'

'And it didn't.'

'Nothing does,' I said, grimacing. 'Have a seat.'

'I'll stand,' she said, inspecting my Van Gogh. 'The name is Monica, by the way.'

'Monica,' I said, taking out the two photographs. 'I have to say, it seems remarkable that you'd expect me to believe your ridiculous story.'

'I haven't told you a story yet.'

'You're going to,' I said, tossing the photographs onto the table. 'A story about time travel and, apparently, a photographer who doesn't know how to use his flash properly.'

'You're a genius, Mister Leeds,' she said, not turning. 'By some certifications I've read, you're the smartest man on the planet. If there had been an obvious flaw – or one that wasn't so obvious – in those photos, you'd have thrown them away. You certainly wouldn't have called me.'

'They're wrong.'

'They . . . ?'

'The people who call me a genius,' I said, sitting down in the chair next to Tobias's. 'I'm not a genius. I'm really quite average.'

'I find that hard to believe.'

'Believe what you will,' I said. 'But I'm *not* a genius. My hallucinations are.'

'Thanks,' J.C. said.

'*Some* of my hallucinations are,' I corrected.

'You accept that the things you see aren't real?' Monica said, turning to me.

'Yes.'

'Yet you talk to them.'

'I wouldn't want to hurt their feelings. Besides, they can be useful.'

'Thanks,' J.C. said.

'*Some* of them can be useful,' I corrected. 'Anyway, they're the reason you're here. You want their minds. Now, tell me your story, Monica, or stop wasting my time.'

She smiled, finally walking over to sit down. 'It's not what you think. There's no time machine.'

'Oh?'

'You don't sound surprised.'

'Time travel into the past is highly, *highly* implausible,' I said. 'Even if it were to have occurred, I'd not know of it, as it would have created a branching path of reality of which I am not a part.'

'Unless this *is* the branched reality.'

'In which case,' I said, 'time travel into the past is still functionally irrelevant to me, as someone who traveled back would create a branching path of which – again – I would not be part.'

'That's one theory, at least,' she said. 'But it's meaningless. As I said, there is no time machine. Not in the conventional sense.'

'So these pictures are fakes?' I asked. 'You're starting to bore me very quickly, Monica.'

She slid three more pictures onto the table.

'Shakespeare,' Tobias said as I held them up one at a time. 'The Colossus of Rhodes. Oh ... now that's clever.'

'Elvis?' I asked.

'Apparently the moment before death,' Tobias said, pointing

to the picture of the waning pop icon sitting in his bathroom, head drooping.

J.C. sniffed. 'As if there isn't anyone around who looks like *that guy.*'

'These are from a camera,' Monica said, leaning forward, 'that takes pictures of the past.'

She paused for dramatic effect. J.C. yawned.

'The problem with each of these,' I said, tossing the pictures onto the table, 'is that they are fundamentally unverifiable. They are pictures of things that have no other visual record to prove them, so therefore small inaccuracies would be impossible to use in debunking.'

'I have seen the device work,' Monica replied. 'It was proven in a rigorous testing environment. We stood in a clean room we had prepared, took cards and drew on the backs of them, and held them up. Then we burned the cards. The inventor of this device entered the room and took photos. Those pictures accurately displayed us standing there, with the cards and the patterns reproduced.'

'Wonderful,' I said. 'Now, if I only had any reason at all to trust your word.'

'You can test the device yourself,' she said. 'Use it to answer any question from history you wish.'

'We could,' Ivy said, 'if it hadn't been stolen.'

'I could do that,' I repeated, trusting what Ivy said. She had good instincts for interrogation, and sometimes fed me lines. 'Except the device has been stolen, hasn't it?'

Monica leaned back in her chair, frowning.

'It wasn't difficult to guess, Steve,' Ivy said. 'She wouldn't be here if everything were working properly, and she'd have brought the camera – to show it off – if she really wanted to prove it to us. I could believe it's in a lab somewhere, too valuable to bring. Only in that case, she'd have invited us to her center of strength, instead of coming to ours.

'She's desperate, despite her calm exterior. See how she keeps tapping the armrest of her chair? Also, notice how she tried to remain standing in the first part of the conversation, looming as if to prop up her authority? She only sat down when she felt awkward with you seeming so relaxed.'

Tobias nodded. '"Never do anything standing that you can do sitting, or anything sitting that you can do lying down." A Chinese proverb, usually attributed to Confucius. Of course, no primary texts from Confucius remain in existence, so nearly everything we attribute to him is guesswork, to some extent or another. Ironically, one of the only things we *are* sure he taught is the Golden Rule – and his quote regarding it is often misattributed to Jesus of Nazareth, who worded the same concept a different way . . .'

I let him speak, the ebbs and flows of his calm voice washing across me like waves. What he was saying wasn't important.

'Yes,' Monica finally said. 'The device was stolen. And that is why I am here.'

'So we have a problem,' I said. 'The only way to prove these pictures authentic for myself would be to have the device. And yet, I can't have the device without doing the work you want me to do – meaning I could easily reach the end of this and discover you've been playing me.'

She dropped one more picture onto the table. A woman in sunglasses and a trench coat, standing in a train station. The picture had been taken from the side as she inspected a monitor above.

Sandra.

'Uh-oh,' J.C. said.

'Where did you get this?' I demanded, standing up.

'I've told you—'

'We're not playing games anymore!' I slammed my hands down on the coffee table. 'Where is she? What do you know?'

Monica drew back, eyes widening. People don't know how to handle schizophrenics. They've read stories, seen films. We make them afraid, though statistically we're not any more likely to commit violent crimes than the average person.

Of course, several people who wrote papers on me claim I'm *not* schizophrenic. Half think I'm making this all up. The other half think I've got something different, something new. Whatever I have – however it is that my brain works – only one person really ever seemed to *get* me. And that was the woman in the picture Monica had just slapped down on the table.

Sandra. In a way, she'd started all of this.

'The picture wasn't hard to get,' Monica said. 'When you used to do interviews, you would talk about her. Obviously, you hoped someone would read the interview and bring you information about her. Maybe you hoped that she would see what you had to say, and return to you . . .'

I forced myself to sit back down.

'You knew she went to the train station,' Monica continued. 'And at what time. You didn't know which train she got on. We started taking pictures until we found her.'

'There must have been a dozen women in that train station with blonde hair and the right look,' I said.

Nobody really knew who she was. Not even me.

Monica took out a sheaf of pictures, a good twenty of them. Each was of a woman. 'We thought the one wearing sunglasses indoors was the most likely choice, but we took a shot of every woman near the right age in the train station that day. Just in case.'

Ivy rested a hand on my shoulder.

'Calmly, Stephen,' Tobias said. 'A strong rudder steers the ship even in a storm.'

I breathed in and out.

'Can I shoot *her*?' J.C. asked.

Ivy rolled her eyes. 'Remind me why we keep him around.'

'Rugged good looks,' J.C. said.

'Listen,' Ivy continued to me. 'Monica undermined her own story. She claims to have only come to you because the camera was stolen – yet how did she get pictures of Sandra without the camera?'

I nodded, clearing my head – with difficulty – and made the accusation to Monica.

Monica smiled slyly. 'We had you in mind for another project. We thought these would be ... handy to have.'

'Darn,' Ivy said, standing right up in Monica's face, focusing on her irises. 'I think she might be telling the truth on that one.'

I stared at the picture. Sandra. It had been almost ten years now. It *still* hurt to think about how she'd left me. Left me, after showing me how to harness my mind's abilities. I ran my fingers across the picture.

'We've got to do it,' J.C. said. 'We've got to look into this, skinny.'

'If there's a chance ...' Tobias said, nodding.

'The camera was probably stolen by someone on the inside,' Ivy guessed. 'Jobs like this one often are.'

'One of your own people took it, didn't they?' I asked.

'Yes,' Monica said. 'But we don't have any idea where they went. We've spent tens of thousands of dollars over the last four days trying to track them. I always suggested you. Other ... factions within our company were against bringing in someone they consider volatile.'

'I'll do it,' I said.

'Excellent. Shall I bring you to our labs?'

'No,' I said. 'Take me to the thief's house.'

'MISTER BALUBAL RAZON,' Tobias read from the sheet of facts as we climbed the stairs. I'd scanned that sheet on the drive over, but had been too deep in thought to give it much specific attention. 'He's ethnically Filipino, but second-generation American. Ph.D. in physics from the University of Maine. No honors. Lives alone.'

We reached the seventh floor of the apartment building. Monica was puffing. She kept walking too close to J.C., which made him scowl.

'I should add,' Tobias said, lowering the sheet of facts, 'Stan informs me that the rain has cleared up before reaching us. We have only sunny weather to look forward to now.'

'Thank goodness,' I said, turning to the door, where two men in black suits stood on guard. 'Yours?' I asked Monica, nodding to them.

'Yeah,' she said. She'd spent the ride over on the phone with some of her superiors.

Monica took out a key to the flat and turned it in the lock. The room inside was a complete disaster. Chinese take-out cartons stood on the windowsill in a row, as if planters intended to grow next year's crop of General Tso's. Books lay in piles everywhere, and the walls were hung with photographs. Not the time-traveling kind, just the ordinary photos a photography buff would take.

We had to shuffle around to get through the door and past the stacks of books. Inside, it was cramped quarters with all of us.

'Wait outside, if you will, Monica,' I said. 'It's kind of tight in here.'

'Tight?' she asked, frowning.

'You keep walking through the middle of J.C.,' I said. 'It's very disturbing for him; he hates being reminded he's a hallucination.'

'I'm not a hallucination,' J.C. snapped. 'I have state-of-the-art stealthing equipment.'

Monica regarded me for a moment, then walked to the doorway, standing between the two guards, hands on hips as she regarded us.

'All right, folks,' I said. 'Have at it.'

'Nice locks,' J.C. said, flipping one of the chains on the door. 'Thick wood, three deadbolts. Unless I miss my guess ...' He poked at what appeared to be a letter box mounted on the wall by the door.

I opened it. There was a pristine handgun inside.

'Ruger Bisley, custom converted to large caliber,' J.C. said with a grunt. I opened the spinning thing that held the bullets and took one out. 'Chambered in .500 Linebaugh,' J.C. continued. 'This is a weapon for a man who knows what he's doing.'

'He left it behind, though,' Ivy said. 'Was he in too much of a hurry?'

'No,' J.C. said. 'This was his door gun. He had a different regular sidearm.'

'Door gun,' Ivy said. 'Is that really a *thing* for you people?'

'You need something with good penetration,' J.C. said, 'that can shoot through the wood when people are trying to force your door. But the recoil of this weapon will do a number on your hand after not too many shots. He would have carried something with a smaller caliber on his person.'

J.C. inspected the gun. 'Never been fired, though. Hmm ... There's a chance someone gave this to him. Perhaps he went to a friend, asked them how to protect himself? A true soldier knows each weapon he owns through repeated firing. No gun fires perfectly straight. Each has a personality.'

'He's a scholar,' Tobias said, kneeling beside the rows of books. 'Historian.'

'You sound surprised,' I said. 'He *does* have a Ph.D. I'd expect him to be smart.'

'He has a Ph.D. in theoretical physics, Stephen,' Tobias said. 'But these are some *very* obscure historical and theological books. Deep reading. It's difficult to be a widely read scholar in more than one area. No wonder he leads a solitary life.'

'Rosaries,' Ivy said; she picked one up from the top of a stack of books, inspecting it. 'Worn, frequently counted. Open one of those books.'

I picked a book up off the floor.

'No, that one. *The God Delusion*.'

'Richard Dawkins?' I said, flipping through it.

'A leading atheist,' Ivy said, looking over my shoulder. 'Annotated with counterarguments.'

'A devout Catholic among a sea of secular scientists,' Tobias said. 'Yes ... many of these works are religious or have religious connotations. Thomas Aquinas, Daniel W. Hardy, Francis Schaeffer, Pietro Alagona ...'

'There's his badge from work,' Ivy said, nodding to something hanging on the wall. It proclaimed, in large letters, *Azari Laboratories, Inc.* Monica's company.

'Call for Monica,' Ivy said. 'Repeat what I tell you.'

'Oh Monica,' I said.

'Am I allowed in now?'

'Depends,' I said, repeating the words Ivy whispered to me. 'Are you going to tell me the truth?'

'About what?'

'About Razon having invented the camera on his own, bringing Azari in only after he had a working prototype.'

Monica narrowed her eyes at me.

'Badge is too new,' I said. 'Not worn or scratched at all from being used or in his pocket. The picture on it can't be more than two months old, judging by the beard he's growing in the badge photo but not in the picture of him at Mount Vernon on his mantle.

'Furthermore, this is *not* the apartment of a high-paid engineer. With a broken elevator? In the northeast quarter of town? Not only is this a rough area, it's too far from your offices. He didn't steal your camera, Monica – though I'm tempted to guess that you're trying to steal it from him. Is that why he ran?'

'He *didn't* come to us with a prototype,' Monica said. 'Not a working one, at least. He had one photo – the one of Washington – and a lot of promises. He needed money to get a stable machine working; apparently, the one he'd built had worked for a few days, then stopped.

'We funded him for eighteen months on a limited access pass to the labs. He received an official badge when he finally got the damn camera working. And he *did* steal it from us.

The contract he signed required all equipment to remain at our laboratories. He used us as a convenient source of cash, then jumped with the prize – wiping all of his data and destroying all other prototypes – as soon as he could get away with it.'

'Truth?' I asked Ivy.

'Can't tell,' she said. 'Sorry. If I could hear a heartbeat … maybe you could put your ear to her chest.'

'I'm sure she'd *love* that,' I said.

J.C. smiled. 'I'm pretty sure *I'd* love that.'

'Oh please,' Ivy said. 'You'd only do it to peek inside her jacket and find out what kind of gun she's carrying.'

'Beretta M9,' J.C. said. 'Already peeked.'

Ivy gave me a glare.

'What?' I said, trying to act innocent. 'He's the one who said it.'

'Skinny,' J.C. put in, 'the M9 is boring, but effective. The way she carries herself says she knows her way around a gun. That puffing she did when climbing the steps? An act. She's far more fit than that. She's trying to pretend she's some kind of manager or paper-pusher at the labs, but she's obviously security of some sort.'

'Thanks,' I told him.

'You,' Monica said, 'are a *very* strange man.'

I focused on her. She'd heard only my parts of the exchange, of course. 'I thought you read my interviews.'

'I did. They don't do you justice. I imagined you as a brilliant mode-shifter, slipping in and out of personalities.'

'That's dissociative identity disorder,' I said. 'It's different.'

'Very good!' Ivy piped in. She'd been schooling me on psychological disorders.

'Regardless,' Monica said. 'I guess I'm just surprised to find out what you really are.'

'Which is?' I asked.

'A middle manager,' she said, looking troubled. 'Anyway, the question remains. Where is Razon?'

'Depends,' I said. 'Does he need to be any place specific to use the camera? Meaning, did he have to *go* to Mount Vernon to take a picture of the past in that location, or can he somehow set the camera to take pictures there?'

'He has to go to the location,' Monica said. 'The camera looks back through time at the exact place you are.'

There were problems with that, but I let them slide for now. Razon. Where would he go? I glanced at J.C., who shrugged.

'You look to him first ?' Ivy said with a flat tone. 'Really.'

I looked to her, and she blushed. 'I . . . I actually don't have anything either.'

J.C. chuckled at that.

Tobias stood up, slow and ponderous, like a distant cloud formation rising into the sky. 'Jerusalem,' he said softly, resting his fingers on a book. 'He's gone to Jerusalem.'

We all looked at him. Well, those of us who could.

'Where else would a believer go, Stephen?' Tobias asked. 'After years of arguments with his colleagues, years of being thought a fool for his faith? This was what it was about all along, this is why he developed the camera. He's gone to answer a question. For us, for himself. A question that has been asked for two thousand years.

'He's gone to take a picture of Jesus of Nazareth – dubbed Christ by his devout – following his resurrection.'

I REQUIRED FIVE first-class seats. This did not sit well with Monica's superiors, many of whom did not approve of me. I met one of those at the airport, a Mr. Davenport. He smelled of pipe smoke, and Ivy critiqued his poor taste in shoes. I thought better of asking him if we could use the corporate jet.

We now sat in the first-class cabin of the plane. I flipped lazily through a thick book on my seat's fold-out tray. Behind me, J.C. bragged to Tobias about the weapons he'd managed to slip past security.

Ivy dozed by the window, with an empty seat next to her. Monica sat beside me, staring at that empty seat. 'So Ivy is by the window?'

'Yes,' I said, flipping a page.

'Tobias and the marine are behind us.'

'J.C.'s a Navy SEAL. He'd shoot you for making that mistake.'

'And the other seat?' she asked.

'Empty,' I said, flipping a page.

She waited for an explanation. I didn't give one.

'So what are you going to do with this camera?' I asked. 'Assuming the thing is real, a fact of which I'm not yet convinced.'

'There are hundreds of applications,' Monica said. 'Law enforcement ... Espionage ... Creating a true account of historical events ... Watching the early formation of the planet for scientific research ...'

'Destroying ancient religions ...'

She raised an eyebrow at me. 'Are you a religious man, then, Mister Leeds?'

'Part of me is.' That was the honest truth.

'Well,' she said. 'Let us assume that Christianity is a sham. Or, perhaps, a movement started by well-meaning people but which has grown beyond proportion. Would it not serve the greater good to expose that?'

'That's not really an argument I'm equipped to enter,' I said. 'You'd need Tobias. He's the philosopher. Of course, I think he's dozing.'

'Actually, Stephen,' Tobias said, leaning between our two seats, 'I'm quite curious about this conversation. Stan is watching our progress, by the way. He says there might be some bumpy weather up ahead.'

'You're looking at something,' Monica said.

'I'm looking at Tobias,' I said. 'He wants to continue the conversation.'

'Can I speak with him?'

'I suppose you can, through me. I'll warn you, though. Ignore anything he says about Stan.'

'Who's Stan?' Monica asked.

'An astronaut that Tobias hears, supposedly orbiting the world in a satellite.' I turned a page. 'Stan is mostly harmless. He gives us weather forecasts, that sort of thing.'

'I ... see,' she said. 'Stan's another one of your special friends?'

I chuckled. 'No. Stan's not real.'

'I thought you said none of them were.'

'Well, true. They're my hallucinations. But Stan is something special. Only Tobias hears him. Tobias is a schizophrenic.'

She blinked in surprise. 'Your hallucination ...'

'Yes?'

'Your hallucination has hallucinations.'

'Yes.'

She settled back, looking disturbed.

'They all have their issues,' I said. 'Ivy is a trypophobic, though she mostly has it under control. Just don't come at her with a wasp's nest. Armando is a megalomaniac. Adoline has OCD.'

'If you please, Stephen,' Tobias said. 'Let her know that I find Razon to be a very brave man.'

I repeated the words.

'And why is that?' Monica asked.

'To be both a scientist and religious is to create an uneasy truce within a man,' Tobias said. 'At the heart of science is accepting only that truth which can be proven. At the heart of faith is to define Truth, at its core, as being unprovable. Razon is a brave man because of what he is doing. Regardless of his discovery, one of two things he holds very dear will be upended.'

'He could be a zealot,' Monica replied. 'Marching blindly forward, trying to find final validation that he has been right all along.'

'Perhaps,' Tobias said. 'But the true zealot would not need validation. The Lord would provide validation. No, I see something else here. A man seeking to meld science and faith, the first person – perhaps in the history of mankind – to *actually* find a way to apply science to the ultimate truths of religion. I find that noble.'

Tobias settled back. I flipped the last few pages of the book as Monica sat in thought. Finished, I stuffed the book into the pocket of the seat in front of me.

Someone rustled the curtains, entering from economy class and coming into the first-class cabin. 'Hello!' a friendly feminine voice said, walking up the aisle. 'I could not help seeing that you had an extra seat up here, and I thought to myself, perhaps they would let me sit in it.'

The newcomer was a round-faced, pleasant young woman in her late twenties. She had tan Indian skin and a deep red dot on her forehead. She wore clothing of intricate make, red and gold, with an Indian shawl-thingy over one shoulder and wrapping around her. I don't know what they're called.

'What's this?' J.C. said. 'Hey, Achmed. You're not going to blow the plane up, are you?'

'My name is Kalyani,' she said. 'And I am most certainly *not* going to blow anything up.'

'Huh,' J.C. said. 'That's disappointing.' He settled back and closed his eyes – or pretended to. He kept one eye cracked toward Kalyani.

'*Why* do we keep him around?' Ivy asked, stretching, coming out of her nap.

'Your head keeps going back and forth,' Monica said. 'I feel like I'm missing entire conversations.'

'You are,' I said. 'Monica, meet Kalyani. A new aspect, and the reason we needed that empty seat.'

Kalyani perkily held out her hand toward Monica, a big grin on her face.

'She can't see you, Kalyani,' I said.

'Oh, right!' Kalyani raised both hands to her face. 'I'm so sorry, Mister Steve. I am very new to this.'

'It's okay. Monica, Kalyani will be our interpreter in Israel.'

'I am a linguist,' Kalyani said, bowing.

'Interpreter ...' Monica said, glancing at the book I'd tucked away. A book of Hebrew syntax, grammar, and vocabulary. 'You just learned Hebrew.'

'No,' I said. 'I glanced through the pages enough to summon

an aspect who speaks it. I'm useless with languages.' I yawned, wondering if there was time left in the flight to pick up Arabic for Kalyani as well.

'Prove it,' Monica said.

I raised an eyebrow toward her.

'I need to see,' Monica said. 'Please.'

With a sigh, I turned to Kalyani. 'How do you say: "I would like to practice speaking Hebrew. Would you speak to me in your language?"'

'Hm ... "I would like to practice speaking Hebrew" is somewhat awkward in the language. Perhaps, "I would like to improve my Hebrew"?'

'Sure.'

'*Ani rotzeh leshapher et ha'ivrit sheli*,' Kalyani said.

'Damn,' I said. 'That's a mouthful.'

'Language!' Ivy called.

'It is not so hard, Mister Steve. Here, try it. *Ani rotzeh leshapher et ha'ivrit sheli*.'

'Any rote zeele shaper hap ... er hav ...' I said.

'Oh my,' Kalyani said. 'That is ... that is very dreadful. Perhaps I will give you one word at a time.'

'Sounds good,' I said, waving over one of the flight attendants, the one who had spoken Hebrew to give the safety information at the start of our flight.

She smiled at us. 'Yes?'

'Uh ...' I said.

'*Ani*,' Kalyani said patiently.

'*Ani*,' I repeated.

'*Rotzeh*.'

'*Rotzeh* ...'

It took a little getting used to, but I made myself known.

The stewardess even congratulated me. Fortunately, translating her words into English was much easier – Kalyani gave me a running translation.

'Oh, your accent is *horrible*, Mister Steve,' Kalyani said as the stewardess moved on. 'I'm so embarrassed.'

'We'll work on it,' I said. 'Thanks.'

Kalyani smiled at me and gave me a hug, then tried to give one to Monica, who didn't notice. Finally, the Indian woman took a seat next to Ivy, and the two began chatting amicably, which was a relief. It always makes my life easier when my hallucinations get along.

'You already spoke Hebrew,' Monica accused. 'You knew it before we started flying, and you spent the last few hours refreshing yourself.'

'Believe that if you want.'

'But it's not *possible*,' she continued. 'A man can't learn an entirely new language in a matter of hours.'

I didn't bother to correct her and say I *hadn't* learned it. If I had, my accent wouldn't have been so horrible, and Kalyani wouldn't have needed to guide me word by word.

'We're on a plane hunting a camera that can take pictures of the past,' I said. 'How is it harder to believe that I just learned Hebrew?'

'Okay, fine. We'll pretend you did that. But if you're capable of learning that quickly, why don't you know every language – every subject, *everything* – by now?'

'There aren't enough rooms in my house for that,' I said. 'The truth is, Monica, I don't *want* any of this. I'd gladly be free of it, so that I could live a more simple life. I sometimes think the lot of them will drive me insane.'

'You . . . aren't insane, then?'

'Heavens no,' I said. I eyed her. 'You don't accept that.'

'You see people who aren't there, Mister Leeds. It's a difficult fact to get around.'

'And yet, I live a good life,' I said. 'Tell me. Why would you consider me insane, but the man who can't hold a job, who cheats on his wife, who can't keep his temper in check? You call *him* sane?'

'Well, perhaps not completely . . .'

'Plenty of "sane" people can't manage to keep it all under control. Their mental state – stress, anxiety, frustration – gets in the way of their ability to be happy. Compared to them, I think I'm downright stable. Though I do admit, it would be nice to be left alone. I don't want to be anyone special.'

'And that's where all of this came from, isn't it?' Monica asked. 'The hallucinations?'

'Oh, you're a psychologist now? Did you read a book on it while we were flying? Where's your new aspect, so I can shake hands with her?'

Monica didn't rise to the bait. 'You create these delusions so that you can foist things off on them. Your brilliance, which you find a burden. Your responsibility – they have to drag you along and make you help people. This lets you pretend, Mister Leeds. Pretend that you are normal. But that's the *real* delusion.'

I found myself wishing the flight would hurry up and be finished.

'I've never heard that theory before,' Tobias said softly from behind. 'Perhaps she has something, Stephen. We should mention it to Ivy—'

'No!' I snapped, turning on him. 'She's dug in my mind enough already.'

I turned back. Monica had that look in her eyes again, the look a 'sane' person gets when they deal with me. It's the look of a person forced to handle unstable dynamite while wearing oven mitts. That look … it hurts far more than the disease itself does.

'Tell me something,' I said to change the topic. 'How'd you let Razon get away with this?'

'It isn't like we didn't take precautions,' Monica said dryly. 'The camera was locked up tightly, but we couldn't very well keep it completely out of the hands of the man we were paying to build it.'

'There's more here,' I said. 'No offense intended, Monica, but you're a sneaky corporate type. Ivy and J.C. figured out ages ago that you're not an engineer. You're either a slimy executive tasked with handling undesirable elements, or you're a slimy security forces leader who does the same.'

'What part of that am I not supposed to take offense at?' she asked coolly.

'How did Razon have access to all of the prototypes?' I continued. 'Surely you copied the design without him knowing. Surely you fed versions of the camera to satellite studios, so they could break them apart and reverse engineer them. I find it quite a stretch to believe he somehow found and destroyed all of those.'

She tapped her armrest for a few minutes. 'None of them work,' she finally admitted.

'You copied the designs exactly?'

'Yes, but we got nothing from it. We asked Razon, and he said that there were still bugs. He always had an excuse, and Razon *did* have trouble with his own prototypes, after all. This is an area of science nobody has breached before. We're the pioneers. Things are bound to have bugs.'

'All true statements,' I said. 'None of which you believe.'

'He was doing *something* to those cameras,' she said. 'Something to make them stop functioning when he wasn't around. He could make any of the prototypes work, given enough time to fiddle. If we swapped in one of our copies during the night, he could make *it* function. Then we'd swap it back, and it wouldn't work for us.'

'Could other people use the cameras in his presence?'

She nodded. 'They could even use them for a little while when he wasn't there. Each camera would always stop working after a short time, and we'd have to bring him back in to fix it. You must understand, Mister Leeds. We only had a few months during which the cameras were working at all. For the majority of his career at Azari, he was considered a complete quack by most.'

'Not by you, I assume.'

She said nothing.

'Without him, without that camera, your career is nothing,' I said. 'You funded him. You championed him. And then, when it finally started working ...'

'He betrayed me,' she whispered.

The look in her eyes was far from pleasant. It occurred to me that if we did find Mr. Razon, I might want to let J.C. at him first. J.C. would probably want to shoot the guy, but Monica wanted to rip him clean apart.

'WELL,' IVY SAID, 'it's a good thing we picked an out-of-the-way city. If we had to find Razon in a large urban center – home to three major world religions, one of the most popular tourist destinations in the world – this would be *really* tough.'

I smiled as we walked out of the airport. One of Monica's two security goons went to track down the cars her company had ordered for us.

My smile didn't do much more than crack the corner of my lips. I hadn't gotten much study done on Arabic during the second half of the flight. I'd spent the time thinking about Sandra. That was never productive.

Ivy watched me from concerned eyes. She could be motherly sometimes. Kalyani strolled over to listen in on some people speaking in Hebrew nearby.

'Ah, Israel,' J.C. said, stepping up to us. 'I've always wanted to come over here, just to see if I could slip through security. They have the best in the world, you know.'

He carried a black duffle on his back that I didn't recognize. 'What's that?'

'M4A1 carbine,' J.C. said. 'With attached advanced combat optical gunsight and M203 grenade launcher.'

'But—'

'I have contacts over here,' he said softly. 'Once a SEAL, always a SEAL.'

The cars arrived, though the drivers seemed bemused at why four people insisted on two cars. As it was, they'd barely fit us all. I got into the second one, with Monica, Tobias, and Ivy – who sat between Monica and me in the back.

'Do you want to talk about it?' Ivy asked softly as she did up her seat belt.

'I don't think we'll find her, even with this,' I said. 'Sandra is good at avoiding attention, and the trail is too cold.'

Monica looked at me, a question on her lips, obviously

thinking I'd been talking to her. It died as she remembered whom she was accompanying.

'There might be a good reason why she left, you know,' Ivy said. 'We don't have the entire story.'

'A good reason? One that explains why, in ten years, she's never contacted us?'

'It's possible,' Ivy said.

I said nothing.

'You're not going to start losing us, are you?' Ivy asked. 'Aspects vanishing? Changing?'

Becoming nightmares. She didn't need to add that last part.

'That won't happen again,' I said. 'I'm in control now.'

Ivy still missed Justin and Ignacio. Honestly, I did too.

'And … this hunt for Sandra,' Ivy said. 'Is it only about your affection for her, or is it about something else?'

'What else could it be about?'

'She was the one who taught you to control your mind.' Ivy looked away. 'Don't tell me you've never wondered. Maybe she has more secrets. A … cure, perhaps.'

'Don't be stupid,' I said. 'I like things how they are.'

Ivy didn't reply, though I could see Tobias looking at me in the car's rearview mirror. Studying me. Judging my sincerity.

Honestly, I was judging my own.

What followed was a long drive to the city – the airport is quite a ways from the city proper. That was followed by a hectic ride through the streets of an ancient – yet modern – city. It was uneventful, save for us almost running over a guy selling olives. At our destination, we piled out of the cars, entering a sea of chattering tourists and pious pilgrims.

Built like a box, the building in front of us had an ancient, simple façade with two large, arched windows on the wall above us. 'The Church of the Holy Sepulchre,' Tobias said. 'Held by tradition to be the site of the crucifixion of Jesus of Nazareth, the structure *also* encloses one of the traditional locations of his burial. This marvelous structure was originally two buildings, constructed in the fourth century by order of Constantine the Great. It replaced a temple to Aphrodite that had occupied the same site for approximately two hundred years.'

'Thank you, Wikipedia,' J.C. grumbled, shouldering his assault rifle. He'd changed into combat fatigues.

'Whether tradition is correct,' Tobias continued calmly, hands clasped behind his back, 'and whether this is the *actual* location of the historical events, is a subject of some dispute. Though tradition has many convenient explanations for anomalies – such as reasoning that the temple to Aphrodite was constructed here to suppress early Christian worship – it has been shown that this church follows the shape of the pagan one in key areas. In addition, the fact that the church lies within the city walls makes for an excellent disputation, as the tomb of Jesus would have been outside the city.'

'It doesn't matter to us whether it is authentic or not,' I said, passing Tobias. 'Razon would have come here. It's one of the most obvious places – if not *the* most obvious place – to start looking. Monica, a word, please.'

She fell into step beside me, her goons going to check if we needed tickets to enter. The security here seemed very heavy – but, then, the church is in the West Bank, and there had been a couple of terrorist scares lately.

'What is it you want?' Monica asked me.

'Does the camera spit out pictures immediately?' I asked. 'Does it give digital results?'

'No. It takes pictures on film only. Medium format, no digital back. Razon insisted it be that way.'

'Now a harder one. You do realize the problems with a camera that takes pictures of one's very location, only farther back in time, don't you?'

'What do you mean?'

'Merely this: we're not in the same location now as we were two thousand years ago. The planet moves. One of the theoretical problems with time travel is that if you were to go back in time a hundred years to the exact point we're standing now, you'd likely find yourself in outer space. Even if you were extremely lucky – and the planet were in the exact same place in its orbit – the Earth's rotation would mean that you'd appear somewhere else on its surface. Or under its surface, or hundreds of feet in the air.'

'That's ridiculous.'

'It's science,' I said, looking up at the face of the church. *What we're doing here is ridiculous.*

And yet ...

'All I know,' she said, 'is that Razon had to go to a place to take pictures of it.'

'All right,' I said. 'One more. What's he like? Personality?'

'Abrasive,' she said immediately. 'Argumentative. And he is *very* protective of his equipment. I'm sure half of the reason he got away with the camera was because he'd repeatedly convinced us he was OCD with his stuff, so we gave him too much leniency.'

Eventually, our group made its way into the church. The stuffy air carried the sounds of whispering tourists and feet shuffling on the stones. It was still a functioning place of worship.

'We're missing something, Steve,' Ivy said, falling into step beside me. 'We're ignoring an important part of the puzzle.'

'Any guesses?' I asked, looking over the highly ornamented insides of the church.

'I'm working on it.'

'Wait,' J.C. said, sauntering up. 'Ivy, you think we're missing something, but you don't know what it is, and have no clue what it might be?'

'Basically,' Ivy said.

'Hey, skinny,' he said to me, 'I think I'm missing a million dollars, but I don't know why, or have any clue as to how I might have earned it. But I'm *really* sure I'm missing it. So if you could do something about that . . .'

'You are such a buffoon,' Ivy said.

'That there, that thing I said,' J.C. continued, 'that was a *metaphor*.'

'No,' she said, 'it was a logical proof.'

'Huh?'

'One intended to demonstrate that you're an idiot. Oh! Guess what? The proof was a success! *Quod erat demonstrandum*. We can accurately say, without equivocation, that you are, indeed, an idiot.'

The two of them walked off, continuing the argument. I shook my head, moving deeper into the church. The place where the crucifixion had supposedly taken place was marked by a gilded alcove, congested with both tourists and the devout. I folded my arms, displeased. Many of the tourists were taking photographs.

'What?' Monica asked me.

'I'd hoped they'd forbid flash photography,' I said. 'Most places like this do.' If Razon had tried to use his, it would have made it more likely that someone had spotted him.

Perhaps it was forbidden, but the security guards standing nearby didn't seem to care what people did.

'We'll start looking,' Monica said, gesturing curtly to her men. The three of them moved through the crowd, going about our fragile plan – which was to try to find someone at one of the holy sites who remembered seeing Razon.

I waited, noticing that a couple of the security guards nearby were chatting in Hebrew. One waved to the other, apparently going off duty, and began to walk away.

'Kalyani,' I said. 'With me.'

'Of course, of course, Mister Steve.' She joined me with a hop in her step as we walked up to the departing guard.

The guard gave me a tired look.

'*Hello,*' I said in Hebrew with Kalyani's help. I'd first mutter under my breath what I wanted to say, so she could translate it for me. '*I apologize for my terrible Hebrew!*'

He paused, then smiled. '*It's not so bad.*'

'*It's dreadful.*'

'*You are Jewish?*' he guessed. '*From the States?*'

'*Actually, I'm not Jewish, though I am from the States. I just think a man should try to learn a country's language before he visits.*'

The guard smiled. He seemed an amiable enough fellow; of course, most people were. And they liked to see foreigners trying their own language. We chatted some more as he walked, and I found that he was indeed going off duty. Someone was coming to pick him up, but he didn't seem to mind talking to me while he waited. I tried to make it obvious that I wanted to practice my language by speaking with a native.

His name was Moshe, and he worked this same shift almost

every day. His job was to watch for people doing stupid things, then stop them – though he confided that his more important duty was to make sure no terrorist strikes happened in the church. He was extra security, not normal staff, hired for the holidays, when the government worried about violence and wanted a more visible presence in tourist sites. This church was, after all, in contested territory.

A few minutes in, I started moving the conversation toward Razon. *'I'm sure you must see some interesting things,'* I said. *'Before we came here, we were at the Garden Tomb. There was this crazy Asian guy there, yelling at everybody.'*

'Yeah?' Moshe asked.

'Yeah. Pretty sure he was American from his accent, but he had Asian features. Anyway, he had this big camera set up on a tripod – as if he were the most important person around, and nobody else deserved to take pictures. Got in this big argument with a guard who didn't want him using his flash.'

Moshe laughed. *'He was here too.'*

Kalyani chuckled after translating that. 'Oh, you're *good*, Mister Steve.'

'Really?' I asked, casually.

'Sure was,' Moshe said. *'Must be the same guy. He was here . . . oh, two days back. Kept cursing out everyone who jostled him, tried to bribe me to move them all away and give him space. Thing is, when he started taking pictures, he didn't mind if anyone stepped in front of him. And he took shots all over the church, even outside, pointed at the dumbest locations!'*

'Real loon, eh?'

'Yes,' the guard said, chuckling. *'I see tourists like him all the time. Big fancy cameras that they spent a ridiculous amount on, but they don't have a bit of photography training. This guy, he didn't*

know when to turn off his flash, you know? Used it on every shot – even out in the sun, and on the altar over there, with all the lights on it!'

I laughed.

'I know!' he said. *'Americans!'* Then he hesitated. *'Oh, uh, no offense meant.'*

'None taken,' I said, relaying immediately what Kalyani said in response. *'I'm Indian.'*

He hesitated, then cocked his head at me.

'Oh!' Kalyani said. 'Oh, I'm sorry, Mister Steve! I wasn't thinking.'

'It's all right.'

The guard laughed. *'You are good at Hebrew, but I do not think that means what you think!'*

I laughed as well, and noticed a woman moving toward him, waving. I thanked him for the conversation, then inspected the church some more. Monica and her flunkies eventually found me, one of them tucking away some photos of Razon. 'Nobody here has seen him, Leeds,' she said. 'This is a dead end.'

'Is that so?' I asked, strolling toward the exit.

Tobias joined us, hands clasped behind his back. 'Such a marvel, Stephen,' he said to me. He nodded toward an armed guard at the doorway. 'Jerusalem, a city whose name literally means "peace." It is filled with islands of serenity like this one, which have seen the solemn worship of men for longer than most countries have existed. Yet here, violence is never more than a few steps away.'

Violence ...

'Monica,' I said, frowning. 'You said you'd searched for Razon on your own, before you came to me. Did that include checking to see if he was on any flights out of the States?'

'Yeah,' she said. 'We have some contacts in Homeland Security. Nobody by Razon's name flew out of the country, but false IDs aren't *that* hard to find.'

'Could a fake passport get you into Israel? One of the most secure countries on the planet?'

She frowned. 'I hadn't thought of that.'

'It seems risky,' I said.

'Well, this is a fine time to bring it up, Leeds. Are you saying he's not here after all? We've wasted—'

'Oh, he's here,' I said absently. 'I found a guard who spoke to him. Razon took pictures all over the place.'

'Nobody we talked to saw him.'

'The guards and clergy in this place see *thousands* of visitors a day, Monica. You can't show them a picture and expect them to remember. You have to focus on something memorable.'

'But—'

'Hush for a moment,' I said, holding up my hand. *He got into the country. A mousy little engineer with extremely valuable equipment, using a fake passport. He had a gun back at his apartment, but hadn't ever fired it. How did he get it?*

Idiot. 'Can you find out when Razon bought that gun?' I asked her. 'Gun laws in the state should make it traceable, right?'

'Sure. I'll look into it when we get to a hotel.'

'Do it now.'

'Now? Do you realize what time it is in the—'

'Do it anyway. Wake people. Get the answers.'

She glared at me, but moved off and made a few phone calls. Some angry conversations followed.

'We should have seen this earlier,' Tobias said, shaking his head.

'I know.'

Eventually, Monica moved back, slapping closed her phone. 'There is no record of Razon buying a gun, ever. The one in his apartment isn't registered anywhere.'

He had help. Of *course* he had help. He'd been planning this for years, and he had access to all those photos to use in proving that he was legitimate.

He'd found someone to supply him. Protect him. Someone who had given him that gun, some fake identification. They'd helped him sneak into Israel.

So whom had he approached? Who was helping him?

'Ivy,' I said. 'We need ...' I trailed off. 'Where's Ivy?'

'No idea,' Tobias said. Kalyani shrugged.

'You've *lost* one of your hallucinations?' Monica asked.

'Yes.'

'Well, summon her back.'

'It doesn't work that way,' I said, and poked through the church, looking around. I got some funny looks from clergy until I finally peeked into a nook and stopped flat.

J.C. and Ivy hastily broke apart from their kissing. Her makeup was mussed, and – incredibly – J.C. had set his gun to the side, ignoring it. That was a first.

'Oh, you've got to be *kidding* me,' I said, raising a hand to my face. '*You two?* What are you doing?'

'I wasn't aware we had to report the nature of our relationship to you,' Ivy said coldly.

J.C. gave me a big thumbs-up and a grin.

'Whatever,' I said. 'Time to go. Ivy, I don't think Razon was working alone. He came into the country on a fake passport, and other factors don't add up. Could he have had some sort of aid here? Maybe a local organization to help him escape suspicion and move in the city?'

'Possible,' she said, hurrying to keep up. 'I would point out it's not *impossible* that he's working alone, but it does seem unlikely, upon consideration. You thought that through on your own? Nice work!'

'Thanks. And your hair is a mess.'

We eventually reached the cars and climbed in, me with Monica, Ivy, and J.C. The two suits and my other aspects took the forward car.

'You could be right on this point,' Monica said as the cars started off.

'Razon is a smart man,' I said. 'He would have wanted allies. It could be another company, perhaps an Israeli one. Do any of your rivals know about this technology?'

'Not that we know of.'

'Steve,' Ivy said, sitting between us. She put her lipstick away, her hair fixed. She was obviously trying to ignore what I'd seen between her and J.C.

Damn, I thought. I'd assumed the two *hated* each other. *Think about that later.* 'Yes?' I asked.

'Ask Monica something for me. Did Razon ever approach her company about a project like this? Taking photos to prove Christianity?'

I relayed the question.

'No,' Monica said. 'If he had, I'd have told you. It would have led us here faster. He never came to us.'

'That's an oddity,' Ivy said. 'The more we work on this case, the more we find that Razon went to incredible lengths in order to come here, to Jerusalem. Why not use the resource he already had? Azari Laboratories.'

'Maybe he wanted freedom,' I said. 'To use his invention as he wished.'

'If that's the case,' Ivy said, 'he wouldn't have approached a rival company, as you proposed. Doing so would have put him back in the same situation. Prod Monica. She looks like she's thinking about something.'

'What?' I asked Monica. 'You have something to add?'

'Well,' Monica said, 'once we knew the camera was working, Razon *did* ask us about some projects he wanted to attempt. Revealing the truth of the Kennedy assassination, debunking or verifying the Patterson-Gimlin bigfoot video, things like that.'

'And you shot him down,' I guessed.

'I don't know if you've spent much time considering the ramifications of this device, Mister Leeds,' Monica said. 'Your questions to me on the plane indicate you've at least started to. Well, we have. And we're terrified.

'This thing will change the world. It's about more than proving mysteries. It means an end to privacy as we know it. If someone can gain access to *any* place where you have *ever* been naked, they can take photos of you in the nude. Imagine the ramifications for the paparazzi.

'Our entire justice system will be upended. No more juries, no more judges, lawyers, or courts. Law enforcement will simply need to go to the scene of the crime and take photos. If you're suspected, you provide an alibi – and they can prove whether or not you were where you claim.'

She shook her head, looking haunted. 'And what of history? National security? Secrets become much harder to keep. States will have to lock down sites where important information was once presented. You won't be able to write things down. A courier carrying sensitive documents has passed down the street? The next day, you can get into just the right position and take a picture *inside* the envelope. We tested that. Imagine having such power. Now imagine every person on the planet having it.'

'Dang,' Ivy whispered.

'So no,' Monica said. 'No, we wouldn't have let Mister Razon go and take photos to prove or disprove Christianity. Not yet. Not until we'd done a *lot* of discussion about the matter. He knew this, I think. It explains why he ran.'

'That didn't stop you from preparing ways to bait me into entering into a business arrangement with you,' I said. 'I suspect if you did it for me, you did it for other important people as well. You've been gathering resources to get yourself some strategic allies, haven't you? Maybe some of the world's rich and elite? To help you ride this wave, once the technology goes out?'

She drew her lips into a line, eyes straight forward.

'That probably looked self-serving to Razon,' I said. 'You won't help him with bringing the truth to mankind, but you'll gather bribery material? Even blackmail material.'

'I'm not at liberty to continue this conversation,' Monica said.

Ivy sniffed. 'Well, we know why he left. I still don't think he'd have gone to a rival company, but he would have gone to *someone*. The Israeli government, maybe? Or—'

Everything went black.

I AWOKE, DAZED. My vision was blurry.

'Explosion,' J.C. said. He crouched beside me. I was ... I was tied up somewhere. In a chair. Hands bound behind me.

'Stay calm, skinny,' J.C. said. '*Calm*. They blew the car in front of us. We swerved. Hit a building at the side of the road. Do you remember?'

I barely did. It was vague.

'Monica?' I croaked, looking about.

She was tied to a chair beside me. Kalyani, Ivy, and Tobias were there as well, tied and gagged. Monica's security men weren't there.

'I managed to crawl free of the wreckage,' J.C. said. 'But I can't get you out.'

'I know,' I said. It was best not to push J.C. on the fact that he was a hallucination. I'm pretty sure he knew, deep down, exactly what he was. He just didn't like admitting it.

'Listen,' J.C. said. 'This is a bad situation, but you *will* keep your head, and you *will* escape alive. Understand, soldier?'

'Yeah.'

'Say it again.'

'*Yes*,' I said, quiet but intense.

'Good man,' J.C. said. 'I'm going to go untie the others.' He moved over, letting my other aspects free.

Monica groaned, shaking her head. 'What ...'

'I think we've made a gross miscalculation,' I said. 'I'm sorry.'

I was surprised at how evenly that came out, considering how terrified I was. I'm an academic at heart – at least, most of my aspects are. I'm not good with violence.

'What do you see?' I asked. This time, my voice quivered.

'Small room,' Ivy said, rubbing her wrists. 'No windows. I

can hear plumbing and faint sounds of traffic outside. We're still in the city.'

'Such lovely places you take us, Stephen,' Tobias said, nodding in thanks as J.C. helped him to his feet. Tobias was getting on in years, now.

'That's Arabic we hear,' Kalyani said. 'And I smell spices. Za'atar, saffron, turmeric, sumac . . . We are near a restaurant, maybe?'

'Yes . . .' Tobias said, eyes closed. 'Soccer stadium, distant. A passing train. Slowing. Stopping . . . Cars, people talking. A mall?' He snapped his eyes open. 'Malha Railway Station. It's the only station in the city near a soccer stadium. This is a busy area. Screaming might draw help.'

'Or might get us killed,' J.C. said. 'Those ropes are tight, skinny. Monica's are too.'

'What's going on?' Monica asked. 'What happened?'

'The pictures,' Ivy said.

I looked at her.

'Monica and her goons showed off those pictures of Razon, walking around the church,' Ivy said. 'They probably asked every person there if they'd seen him. If he *was* working with someone . . .'

I groaned. Of course. Razon's allies would have been watching for anyone hunting him. Monica had drawn a big red bull's-eye on us.

'All right,' I said. 'J.C. You're going to have to get us out of this. What should—'

The door opened.

I immediately turned toward our captors. I didn't find what I'd expected. Instead of Islamic terrorists of some sort, we were faced by a group of Filipino men in suits.

'Ah …' Tobias said.

'Mister Leeds,' said the man in the front, speaking with an accented voice. He flipped through a folder full of papers. 'By all accounts, you are a very interesting and very … reasonable person. We apologize for your treatment so far, and would like to see you placed in much more comfortable conditions.'

'I sense a deal coming on,' Ivy warned.

'I am called Salic,' the man said. 'I represent a certain group with interests that may align with your own. Have you heard of the MNLF, Mister Leeds?'

'The Moro National Liberation Front,' Tobias said. 'It is a Filipino revolutionary group seeking to split off and create its own nation-state.'

'I've heard of it,' I said.

'Well,' Salic said. 'I have a proposal for you. We have the device for which you are searching, but we have run into some difficulties in operating it. How much would it cost us to enlist your aid?'

'One million, US,' I said without missing a beat.

'Traitor!' Monica sputtered.

'You aren't even paying me, Monica,' I said, amused. 'You can't blame me for taking a better deal.'

Salic smiled. He fully believed I'd sell out Monica. Sometimes it is very useful to have a reputation for being a reclusive, amoral jerk.

The thing is, I'm really only the reclusive part. And maybe, admittedly, the jerk part. When you have that mix, people generally assume you don't have morals either.

'The MNLF is a paramilitary organization,' Tobias continued. 'There hasn't been much in the way of violence on their part, however, so this is surprising to see. Their fundamental difference with the main Filipino government is over religion.'

'Isn't it always?' J.C. said with a grunt, inspecting the newcomers for weapons. 'This guy is packing,' he said, nodding to the leader. 'I think they all are.'

'Indeed,' Tobias said. 'Think of the MNLF as the Filipino version of the IRA, or Palestine's own Hamas. The latter may be a more accurate comparison, as the MNLF is often seen as an Islamic organization. Most of the Philippines is Roman Catholic, but the Bangsamoro region – where the MNLF operates – is predominantly Islamic.'

'Untie him,' Salic said, gesturing toward me.

His men got to work.

'He's lying about something,' Ivy said.

'Yes,' Tobias said. 'I think ... Yes, he's not MNLF. He's perhaps trying to pin this on them. Stephen, the MNLF is *very much* against endangering civilians. It's really quite remarkable, if you read about them. They are freedom fighters, but they have a strict code of whom they'll hurt. They have recently been dedicated to peaceful secession.'

'That must not make them terribly popular with all who would follow them,' I said. 'Are there splinter groups?'

'What is that?' Salic asked.

'Nothing,' I said, standing up, rubbing my wrists. 'Thank you. I would *very much* like to see the device.'

'This way, please,' Salic said.

'Bastard,' Monica called after me.

'Language!' Ivy said, pursing her lips. She and my other aspects followed me out, and the guards shut the door on Monica, leaving her alone in the room.

'Yes ...' Tobias said, walking behind the men who escorted

me up the steps. 'Stephen, I think this is the Abu Sayyaf. Led by a man named Khadaffy Janjalani, they split from the MNLF because the organization wasn't willing to go far enough. Janjalani died recently, and the future of the movement is somewhat in doubt, but his goal was to create a purely Islamic state in the region. He considered the killing of anyone opposed to him as an ... elegant way to achieve his goals.'

'Sounds like we have a winner,' J.C. said. 'All right, skinny. Here's what you need to do. Kick the guy behind you as he's taking a step. He'll fall into the fellow next to him, and you can tackle Salic. Spin him around to cover gunfire from behind, take his weapon from inside his coat, and start firing through his body at the men down there.'

Ivy looked sick. 'That's awful!'

'You don't think he's going to let us go, do you?' J.C. asked.

'The Abu Sayyaf,' Tobias said helpfully, 'has been the source of numerous killings, bombings, and kidnappings in the Philippines. They also are *very* brutal with the locals, acting as more of an organized crime family than true revolutionaries.'

'So ... that would be a no, eh?' J.C. said.

We reached the ground floor, and Salic led us into a side room. Two more men were here, outfitted as soldiers, with grenades on their belts and assault rifles in their hands.

Between them, on the table, was a medium format camera. It looked ... ordinary.

'I need Razon here,' I said, sitting down. 'To ask him questions.'

Salic sniffed. 'He will not speak to you, Mister Leeds. You can trust us on this count.'

'So he's not working with them?' J.C. asked. 'I'm confused.'

'Bring him anyway,' I said, and carefully began prodding at the camera.

Thing is, I had *no* idea what I was doing. *Why, WHY didn't I bring Ivans with me?* I should have known I'd need a mechanic on this trip.

But if I brought too many aspects – kept too many of them around me at once – bad things happened. That was immaterial, now. Ivans was a continent away.

'Anyone?' I asked under my breath.

'Don't look at me,' Ivy said. 'I can't get the remote control to work half the time.'

'Cut the red wire,' J.C. said. 'It's always the red wire.'

I gave him a flat stare, then unscrewed one part of the camera in an attempt to look like I knew what I was doing. My hands were shaking.

Salic, fortunately, sent someone to do as I requested. After that, he watched me carefully. He'd probably read about the Longway Incident, where I'd disassembled, fixed, and reassembled a complex computer system in time to stop a detonation. But that had all been Ivans, with some aid by Chin, our resident computer expert.

Without them, I was useless at this sort of thing. I tried my best to look otherwise until the soldier brought back Razon. I recognized him from the pictures Monica had shown me. Barely. His lip was cracked and bleeding, his left eye puffy, and he walked with a stumbling limp. As he sat down on a stool near me, I saw that he was missing one hand. The stump was wrapped with a bloody rag.

He coughed. 'Ah. Mister Leeds, I believe,' he said with a faint Filipino accent. 'I'm terribly sorry to find you here.'

'Careful,' Ivy said, inspecting Razon. She was standing

right beside him. 'They're watching. Don't act too friendly.'

'Oh, I do *not* like this at all,' Kalyani said. She'd moved over to some crates at the back of the room, crouching down for cover. 'Is it often going to be like this around you, Mister Steve? Because I am not very well cut out for this.'

'You're *sorry* to find me here?' I said to Razon, making my voice harsh. 'Sorry, but not surprised. You're the one who helped Monica and her cronies get blackmail material on me.'

His unswollen eye widened a fraction. He knew it hadn't been blackmail material. Or so I hoped. Would he see? Would he realize I was here to help him?

'I did that ... under duress,' he said.

'You're still a bastard, so far as I'm concerned,' I spat.

'Language!' Ivy said, hands on hips.

'Bah,' I said to Razon. 'It doesn't matter. You're going to show me how to make this machine work.'

'I will not!' he said.

I turned a screw, my mind racing. How could I get close enough to speak to him quietly, but not draw suspicion? 'You will, or—'

'Careful, you fool!' Razon said, leaping from his chair.

One of the soldiers leveled a gun at us.

'Safety's on,' J.C. said. 'Nothing to be worried about. Yet.'

'This is a very delicate piece of equipment,' Razon said, taking the screwdriver from me. 'You mustn't break it.' He started screwing with his good arm. Then, speaking very softly, he continued. 'You are here with Monica?'

'Yes.'

'She is not to be trusted,' he said. Then paused. 'But she

never beat me or cut my hand off. So perhaps I am not one to speak on whom to trust.'

'How did they take you?' I whispered.

'I bragged to my mother,' he said. 'And she bragged to her family. It got to these monsters. They have contacts in Israel.' He wavered, and I reached to steady him. His face was pale. This man was *not* in good shape.

'They sent to me,' he said, forcing himself to keep screwing. 'They claimed to be Christian fundamentalists from my country, eager to fund my operation to find proof. I did not find out the truth until two days ago. It—'

He cut off, dropping the screwdriver as Salic stepped closer to us. The terrorist waved, and one of his soldiers grabbed Razon and jerked him back by his bloodied arm. Razon cried out in pain.

The soldiers proceeded to throw him to the ground and beat him with the butts of their rifles. I watched in horror, and Kalyani began crying. Even J.C. turned away.

'I am not a monster, Mister Leeds,' Salic said, squatting down beside my chair. 'I am a man with few resources. You will find that the two are quite difficult to differentiate, in most situations.'

'Please stop the soldiers,' I whispered.

'I am *trying* to find a peaceful solution, you see,' Salic said. He did not stop the beating. 'My people are condemned when we use the only methods we have – the methods of the desperate – to fight. These are the methods that every revolutionary, including the founders of your own country, has used to gain freedom. We will kill if we have to, but perhaps we do not have to. Here on this table we have peace, Mister Leeds. Fix this machine, and you will save thousands upon thousands of lives.'

'Why do you want it?' I said, frowning. 'What is it to you? Power to blackmail?'

'Power to fix the world,' Salic said. 'We just need a few photos. Proof.'

'Proof that Christianity is false, Stephen,' Tobias said, walking up beside me. 'That will be a difficult task for them, as Islam accepts Jesus of Nazareth as a prophet. They do not accept the resurrection, however, or many of the miracles attributed to later followers. With the right photo, they could try to undermine Catholicism – the religion followed by most Filipinos – and therefore destabilize the region.'

I'll admit that, strangely, I was tempted. Oh, not tempted to help a monster like Salic. But I did see his point. Why not take this camera, prove *all* religions false?

It would cause chaos. Perhaps a great deal of death, in some parts of the world.

Or would it?

'Faith is not so easily subverted,' Ivy said dismissively. 'This wouldn't cause the problems he thinks it would.'

'Because faith is blind?' Tobias asked. 'Perhaps you are right. Many would continue to believe, despite the facts.'

'What facts?' Ivy said. 'Some pictures that may or may not be trustworthy? Produced by a science nobody understands?'

'Already you try to protect that which has yet to be discounted,' Tobias said calmly. 'You act as if you know what will happen, and need to be defensive about the proof that *may* be found. Ivy, don't you see? What facts would it take to make you look at things with rational eyes? How can you be so logical in so many areas, yet be so blind in this one?'

'Quiet!' I said to them. I raised my hands to my head. 'Quiet!'

Salic frowned at me. Only then did he notice what his soldiers had done to Razon.

He shouted something in Tagalog, or perhaps one of the other Filipino languages – maybe I should have studied those instead of Hebrew. The soldiers backed away, and Salic knelt to roll over the fallen Razon.

Razon snapped his good hand into Salic's jacket, reaching for the gun. Salic jumped back, and one of the soldiers cried out. A single quiet *click* followed.

Everyone in the room grew still. One of the soldiers had taken out a handgun with a suppressor on it and shot Razon in a panic. The scientist lay back, dead eyes staring open, Salic's handgun slipping from his fingers.

'Oh, that poor man,' Kalyani said, moving over to kneel beside him.

At that moment, someone tackled one of the soldiers by the door, pulling him down from behind.

Shouting began immediately. I jumped out of my chair, reaching for the camera. Salic got it first, slamming one hand down on it, then reached toward his gun on the floor.

I cursed, scrambling away, throwing myself behind the stack of crates where Kalyani had taken cover a few moments before. Gunfire erupted in the room, and one of the crates near me threw up chips as a shot hit it.

'It's Monica!' Ivy said, taking cover beside the desk. 'She got out, and she's attacking them.'

I dared peek around, in time to see one of the Abu Sayyaf suits fall to gunfire, toppling in the center of the room near Razon's body. The others fired at Monica, who'd taken cover in the stairwell that led down to where we'd been captive.

'Holy hell!' J.C. said, crouching beside me. 'She escaped

on her own. I think I might have to start liking that woman!'

Salic yelled in Tagalog. He hadn't come after me, but had taken cover near his guards. He clutched the camera close, and was joined by two other soldiers as they ran down the stairs from above.

This gunfire would draw attention soon, I guessed. Not soon enough. They had Monica pinned. I could barely see her, hiding in her stairwell, trying to find a way to get out and fire on the men with the weapon she'd stolen from the guard she'd tackled. His feet stuck out of the doorway near her.

'Okay, skinny,' J.C. said. 'This is your chance. Something has to be done. They'll get her before help comes, and we lose the camera. It's hero time.'

'I . . .'

'You could run, Stephen,' Tobias said. 'There's a room right behind us. There will be windows. I'm not saying you should do it; I'm giving you the options.'

Kalyani whimpered, huddled down in the corner. Ivy lay under a table, fingers in her ears, watching the fire-fight with calculating eyes.

Monica tried to duck out and fire, but bullets tore into the wall beside her, forcing her back. Salic was still yelling something. Several of the soldiers started firing on me, driving me back under cover.

Bullets popped against the wall above me, chips of stone dropping on my head. I breathed in and out. 'I can't do this, J.C.'

'You can,' he said. 'Look, they're carrying grenades. Did you see those on the belts of the soldiers? One will get smart, toss one of those down the stairwell, and Monica's gone. Dead.'

If I let them keep the camera – that kind of power, in the hands of men like this . . .

Monica yelled.

'She's hit!' Ivy called.

I scrambled out from behind the crates and ran for the fallen soldier at the center of the room. He'd dropped a handgun. Salic noticed me as I grabbed the weapon and raised it. My hands shook, quivering.

This is never going to work. I can't do this. It's impossible.

I'm going to die.

'Don't worry, kid,' J.C. said, taking my wrist in his own. 'I've got this.'

He pulled my arm to the side and I fired, barely looking, then he moved the gun in a series of motions, pausing just briefly for me to pull the trigger each time. It was over in moments.

Each of the armed men dropped. The room went completely still. J.C. released my wrist, and my arm fell leaden at my side.

'Did *we* do that?' I asked, looking at the fallen men.

'Damn,' Ivy said, unplugging her ears. 'I *knew* there was a reason we kept you around, J.C.'

'Language, Ivy,' he said, grinning.

I dropped the pistol – probably not the smartest thing I've ever done, but then again, I wasn't exactly in my right mind. I hurried to Razon's side. He had no pulse. I closed his eyes, but left the smile on his lips.

This was what he'd wanted. He'd wanted them to kill him so that he couldn't be forced to give up his secrets. I sighed. Then, checking a theory, I shoved my hand into his pocket.

Something pricked my fingers, and I brought them out bloodied. 'What . . . ?'

I hadn't expected *that*.

'Leeds?' Monica's voice said.

I looked up. She was standing in the doorway to the room, holding her shoulder, which was bloodied. 'Did *you* do this?'

'J.C. did it,' I said.

'Your hallucination? Shot these men?'

'Yes. No. I . . .' I wasn't sure. I stood up and walked over to Salic, who had been hit square in the forehead. I leaned down and picked up the camera, then twisted one piece of it, my back to Monica.

'Uh . . . Mister Steve?' Kalyani said, pointing. 'I do not think that one is dead. Oh my.'

I looked. One of the guards I'd shot was turning over. He held something in a bloodied hand.

A grenade.

'Out!' I yelled at Monica, grabbing her by the arm as I charged out of the room.

The detonation hit me from behind like a crashing wave.

EXACTLY ONE MONTH later, I sat in my mansion, drinking a cup of lemonade. My back ached, but the shrapnel wounds were healing. It hadn't been that bad.

Monica did not give the cast on her arm much notice. She held her own cup, seated in the room where I'd first met her.

Her offer today had not been unexpected.

'I'm afraid,' I said, 'you've come to the wrong person. I must refuse.'

'I see,' Monica said.

'She's been working on her scowl,' J.C. said appreciatively from where he leaned against the wall. 'It's getting better.'

'If you would *look* at the camera ...' Monica said.

'When I saw it last, it was in at least sixteen pieces,' I said. 'There's just not anything to work with.'

She narrowed her eyes at me. She still suspected I'd dropped it on purpose as the explosion hit. It didn't help that Razon's body had been burned to near unrecognizability in the subsequent explosions and fire that had consumed the building. Any items he'd had on him – secrets that explained how the camera *really* worked – had been destroyed.

'I'll admit,' I said, leaning forward, 'that I'm not terribly sorry to discover you can't fix the thing. I'm not certain the world is prepared for the information it could provide.' *Or, at least, I'm not certain the world is prepared for people like you controlling that information.*

'But—'

'Monica, I don't know what I could do that your engineers haven't. We're simply going to have to accept the fact that this technology died with Razon. If what he did was anything other than a hoax. To be honest, I'm increasingly certain it was one. Razon was tortured beyond what a simple scientist could have endured, yet did not give the terrorists what they wanted. It was because he couldn't. It was all a sham.'

She sighed and stood up. 'You are passing up on greatness, Mister Leeds.'

'My dear,' I said, standing, 'you should know by now that I've already *had* greatness. I traded it for mediocrity and some measure of sanity.'

'You should ask for a refund,' she said. 'Because I'm not certain I have found either in you.' She took something from her pocket and dropped it on the table. A large envelope.

'And this is?' I asked, taking it.

'We found film in the camera,' she said. 'Only one image was recoverable.'

I hesitated, then slipped the picture out. It was in black and white, like the others. It depicted a man, bearded and robed, sitting – though on what, I couldn't see. His face was striking. Not because of its shape, but because it was looking *directly* at the camera. A camera that wouldn't be there for two thousand years.

'We think it comes from the Triumphal Entry,' she said. 'The background, at least, looks to be the Beautiful Gate. It's hard to tell.'

'My God,' Ivy whispered, stepping up beside me.

Those eyes … I stared at the photo. Those *eyes*.

'Hey, I thought we weren't supposed to swear around you,' J.C. called to Ivy.

'It wasn't a curse,' she said, resting her fingers reverently on the photo. 'It was an identification.'

'It's meaningless, unfortunately,' Monica said. 'There's no way to prove who that is. Even if we could, it wouldn't do anything toward proving or disproving Christianity. This was before the man was killed. Of all the shots for Razon to get …' She shook her head.

'It doesn't change my mind,' I said, slipping the photo back into the envelope.

'I didn't think it would,' Monica said. 'Consider it as payment.'

'I didn't end up accomplishing much for you.'

'Nor we for you,' she said, walking from the room. 'Good evening, Mister Leeds.'

I rubbed my finger on the envelope, listening as Wilson showed Monica to the door, then shut it. I left Ivy and J.C. having a conversation about his cursing, then walked into the entryway and up the stairs. I wound around them, hand on the banister, before reaching the upper hallway.

My study was at the end. The room was lit by a single lamp on the desk, the shades drawn against the night. I walked to my desk and sat down. Tobias sat in one of the two other chairs beside it.

I picked up a book – the last in what had been a huge stack – and began leafing through. The picture of Sandra, the one recovered from the train station, hung tacked to the wall beside me.

'Have they figured it out?' Tobias asked.

'No,' I said. 'Have you?'

'It was never the camera, was it?'

I smiled, turning a page. 'I searched his pockets right after he died. Something cut my fingers. Broken glass.'

Tobias frowned. Then, after a moment's thought, he smiled. 'Shattered lightbulbs?'

I nodded. 'It wasn't the camera, it was the *flash*. When Razon took pictures at the church, he used the flash even outside in the sunlight. Even when his subject was well lit, even when he was trying to capture something that happened during the day, such as Jesus' appearance outside the tomb following his resurrection. That's a mistake a good photographer wouldn't make. And he was a good photographer, judging by the pictures hung in his apartment. He had a good eye for lighting.'

I turned a page, then reached into my pocket and took something out, setting it on the table. A detachable flash, the one I'd taken off the camera just before the explosion. 'I'm not sure if it's something about the flash mechanism or the bulbs, but I do know he was swapping out the bulbs in order to stop the thing from working when he didn't want it to.'

'Beautiful,' Tobias said.

'We'll see,' I replied. 'This flash doesn't work; I've tried. I don't know what's wrong with it. You know how the cameras would work for Monica's people for a while? Well, many camera flashes have multiple bulbs like this one. I suspect that only one of these had anything to do with the temporal effects. The special bulbs burned out quickly, after maybe ten shots.'

I turned a few pages.

'You're changing, Stephen,' Tobias finally said. 'You noticed this without Ivy. Without any of us. How long before you don't need us any longer?'

'I hope that never happens,' I said. 'I don't want to be that man.'

'And yet you chase *her*.'

'And yet I do,' I whispered.

One step closer. I knew what train Sandra had taken. A ticket peeked out of her coat pocket. I could make out the numbers, just barely.

She'd gone to New York. For ten years, I'd been hunting this answer – which was only a tiny fraction of a much larger hunt. The trail was a decade old, but it was *something*.

For the first time in years, I was making progress. I closed the book and sat back, looking up at Sandra's picture. She was beautiful. So very beautiful.

Something rustled in the dark room. Neither Tobias nor I stirred as a short, balding man sat down at the desk's empty chair. 'My name is Arnaud,' he said. 'I'm a physicist specializing in temporal mechanics, causality, and quantum theories. I believe you have a job for me?'

I set the final book on the stack of those I'd read during the last month. 'Yes, Arnaud,' I said. 'I do.'

ACKNOWLEDGMENTS

As always, my wonderful wife Emily gets a big thumbs-up for dealing with the sometimes erratic life of a professional writer. The incumbent Peter Ahlstrom did quite a bit of special work on this project. Another person of note is Moshe Feder, who gave me one of my very early reads on this book – and who discussed thoughts, possibilities, and conjectures regarding it from its earliest days.

My agent, Joshua Bilmes, has been his usual awesome self. Other early readers include Brian T. Hill, Dominique Nolan, Kaylynn ZoBell, Ben Olsen, Danielle Olsen, Karen Ahlstrom, Dan Wells, Alan Layton, and Ethan Skarstedt.

A special thanks to Subterranean Press for giving this work a place in print. Bill Schafer and Yanni Kuznia have been fantastic.

Brandon Sanderson

THE EMPEROR'S SOUL

For Lucie Tuan and Sherry Wang,
who provided inspiration.

PROLOGUE

GAOTONA RAN HIS fingers across the thick canvas, inspecting one of the greatest works of art he had ever seen. Unfortunately, it was a lie.

'The woman is a danger.' Hissed voices came from behind him. 'What she does is an abomination.'

Gaotona tipped the canvas toward the hearth's orange-red light, squinting. In his old age, his eyes weren't what they had once been. *Such precision,* he thought, inspecting the brush strokes, feeling the layers of thick oils. Exactly like those in the original.

He would never have spotted the mistakes on his own. A blossom slightly out of position. A moon that was just a sliver too low in the sky. It had taken their experts days of detailed inspection to find the errors.

'She is one of the best Forgers alive.' The voices belonged to Gaotona's fellow arbiters, the empire's most important bureaucrats. 'She has a reputation as wide as the empire. We need to execute her as an example.'

'No.' Frava, leader of the arbiters, had a sharp, nasal voice. 'She is a valuable tool. This woman can save us. We must use her.'

Why? Gaotona thought again. *Why would someone capable of this artistry, this majesty, turn to forgery? Why not create original paintings? Why not be a true artist?*

I must understand.

'Yes,' Frava continued, 'the woman is a thief, and she practices a horrid art. But I can control her, and with her talents we can fix this mess we have found ourselves in.'

The others murmured worried objections. The woman they spoke of, Wan ShaiLu, was more than a simple con artist. So much more. She could change the nature of reality itself. That raised another question. Why would she bother learning to paint? Wasn't ordinary art mundane compared to her mystical talents?

So many questions. Gaotona looked up from his seat beside the hearth. The others stood in a conspiratorial clump around Frava's desk, their long, colorful robes shimmering in the firelight. 'I agree with Frava,' Gaotona said.

The others glanced at him. Their scowls indicated they cared little for what he said, but their postures told a different tale. Their respect for him was buried deep, but it was remembered.

'Send for the Forger,' Gaotona said, rising. 'I would hear what she has to say. I suspect she will be more difficult to control than Frava claims, but we have no choice. We either use this woman's skill, or we give up control of the empire.'

The murmurs ceased. How many years had it been since Frava and Gaotona had agreed on anything at all, let alone on something so divisive as making use of the Forger?

One by one, the other three arbiters nodded.

'Let it be done,' Frava said softly.

DAY TWO

SHAI PRESSED HER fingernail into one of the stone blocks of her prison cell. The rock gave way slightly. She rubbed the dust between her fingers. Limestone. An odd material for use in a prison wall, but the whole wall wasn't of limestone, merely that single vein within the block.

She smiled. Limestone. That little vein had been easy to miss, but if she was right about it, she had finally identified all forty-four types of rock in the wall of her circular pit of a prison cell. Shai knelt down beside her bunk, using a fork – she'd bent back all of the tines but one – to carve notes into the wood of one bed leg. Without her spectacles, she had to squint as she wrote.

To Forge something, you had to know its past, its nature. She was almost ready. Her pleasure quickly slipped away, however, as she noticed another set of markings on the bed leg, lit by her flickering candle. Those kept track of her days of imprisonment.

So little time, she thought. If her count was right, only a day remained before the date set for her public execution.

Deep inside, her nerves were drawn as tight as strings on an instrument. One day. One day remaining to create a soul-stamp and escape. But she had no soul-stone, only a crude piece of wood, and her only tool for carving was a fork.

It would be incredibly difficult. That was the point. This cell was meant for one of her kind, built of stones with many different veins of rock in them to make them difficult to Forge. They would come from different quarries and each have unique histories. Knowing as little as she did, Forging them would be nearly impossible. And even if she did transform the rock, there was probably some other fail safe to stop her.

Nights! What a mess she'd gotten herself into.

Notes finished, she found herself looking at her bent fork. She'd begun carving the wooden handle, after prying off the metal portion, as a crude soulstamp. *You're not going to get out this way, Shai*, she told herself. *You need another method.*

She'd waited six days, searching for another way out. Guards to exploit, someone to bribe, a hint about the nature of her cell. So far, nothing had—

Far above, the door to the dungeons opened.

Shai leaped to her feet, tucking the fork handle into her waistband at the small of her back. Had they moved up her execution?

Heavy boots sounded on the steps leading into the dungeon, and she squinted at the newcomers who appeared above her cell. Four were guards, accompanying a man with long features and fingers. A Grand, the race who led the empire. That robe of blue and green indicated a minor functionary who had passed the tests for government service, but not risen high in its ranks.

Shai waited, tense.

The Grand leaned down to look at her through the grate. He paused for just a moment, then waved for the guards to unlock it. 'The arbiters wish to interrogate you, Forger.'

Shai stood back as they opened her cell's ceiling, then lowered a ladder. She climbed, wary. If *she* were going to take someone to an early execution, she'd have let the prisoner think something else was happening, so she wouldn't resist. However, they didn't lock Shai in manacles as they marched her out of the dungeons.

Judging by their route, they did indeed seem to be taking her toward the arbiters' study. Shai composed herself. A new challenge, then. Dared she hope for an opportunity? She shouldn't have been caught, but she could do nothing about that now. She had been bested, betrayed by the Imperial Fool when she'd assumed she could trust him. He had taken her copy of the Moon Scepter and swapped it for the original, then run off.

Shai's Uncle Won had taught her that being bested was a rule of life. No matter how good you were, someone was better. Live by that knowledge, and you would never grow so confident that you became sloppy.

Last time she had lost. This time she would win. She abandoned all sense of frustration at being captured and became the person who could deal with this new chance, whatever it was. She would seize it and thrive.

This time, she played not for riches, but for her life.

The guards were Strikers – or, well, that was the Grand name for them. They had once called themselves Mulla'dil, but their nation had been folded into the empire so long ago that few used the name. Strikers were a tall people with a lean musculature and pale skin. They had hair almost as dark as Shai's, though theirs curled while hers lay straight and long. She tried with some success not to feel dwarfed by them. Her people, the MaiPon, were not known for their stature.

'You,' she said to the lead Striker as she walked at the front of the group. 'I remember you.' Judging by that styled hair, the youthful captain did not often wear a helmet. Strikers were well regarded by the Grands, and their Elevation was not unheard of. This one had a look of eagerness to him. That polished armor, that crisp air. Yes, he fancied himself bound for important things in the future.

'The horse,' Shai said. 'You threw me over the back of your horse after I was captured. Tall animal, Gurish descent, pure white. Good animal. You know your horseflesh.'

The Striker kept his eyes forward, but whispered under his breath, 'I'm going to enjoy killing you, woman.'

Lovely, Shai thought as they entered the Imperial Wing of the palace. The stonework here was marvelous, after the ancient Lamio style, with tall pillars of marble inlaid with reliefs. Those large urns between the pillars had been created to mimic Lamio pottery from long ago.

Actually, she reminded herself, *the Heritage Faction still rules, so . . .*

The emperor would be from that faction, as would the council of five arbiters who did much of the actual ruling. Their faction lauded the glory and learning of past cultures, even going so far as to rebuild their wing of the palace as an imitation of an ancient building. Shai suspected that on the bottoms of those 'ancient' urns would be soulstamps that had transformed them into perfect imitations of famous pieces.

Yes, the Grands called Shai's powers an abomination, but the only aspect of it that was technically illegal was creating a Forgery to change a person. Quiet Forgery of objects was allowed, even exploited, in the empire so long as the Forger was carefully controlled. If someone were to turn over one of those urns and remove the stamp on the bottom, the piece would become simple unornamented pottery.

The Strikers led her to a door with gold inlay. As it opened, she managed to catch a glimpse of the red soulstamp on the bottom inside edge, transforming the door into an imitation of some work from the past. The guards ushered her into a homey room with a crackling hearth, deep rugs, and stained wood furnishings. *Fifth century hunting lodge*, she guessed.

All five arbiters of the Heritage Faction waited inside. Three – two women, one man – sat in tall-backed chairs at the hearth. One other woman occupied the desk just inside the doors: Frava, senior among the arbiters of the Heritage Faction, was probably the most powerful person in the empire other than Emperor Ashravan himself. Her greying hair was woven into a long braid with gold and red ribbons; it draped a robe of matching gold. Shai had long pondered how to rob this woman, as – among her duties – Frava oversaw the Imperial Gallery and had offices adjacent to it.

Frava had obviously been arguing with Gaotona, the elderly male Grand standing beside the desk. He stood up straight and clasped his hands behind his back in a thoughtful pose. Gaotona was eldest of the ruling arbiters. He was said to be the least influential among them, out of favor with the emperor.

Both fell silent as Shai entered. They eyed her as if she were a cat that had just knocked over a fine vase. Shai missed her spectacles, but took care not to squint as she stepped up to face these people; she needed to look as strong as possible.

'Wan ShaiLu,' Frava said, reaching to pick up a sheet of paper from the desk. 'You have quite the list of crimes credited to your name.'

The way you say that . . . What game was this woman playing? *She wants something of me*, Shai decided. *That is the only reason to bring me in like this.*

The opportunity began to unfold.

'Impersonating a noblewoman of rank,' Frava continued, 'breaking into the palace's Imperial Gallery, reForging your soul, and of course the attempted theft of the Moon Scepter. Did you really assume that we would fail to recognize a simple forgery of such an important imperial possession?'

Apparently, Shai thought, *you have done just that, assuming that the Fool escaped with the original.* It gave Shai a little thrill of satisfaction to know that her forgery now occupied the Moon Scepter's position of honor in the Imperial Gallery.

'And what of this?' Frava said, waving long fingers for one of the Strikers to bring something from the side of the room. A painting, which the guard placed on the desk. Han ShuXen's masterpiece *Lily of the Spring Pond*.

'We found this in your room at the inn,' Frava said, tapping her fingers on the painting. 'It is a copy of a painting I myself own, one of the most famous in the empire. We gave it to our assessors, and they judge that your forgery was amateur at best.'

Shai met the woman's eyes.

'Tell me why you have created this forgery,' Frava said, leaning forward. 'You were obviously planning to swap this for the painting in my office by the Imperial Gallery. And yet, you were striving for the *Moon Scepter* itself. Why plan to steal the painting too? Greed?'

'My uncle Won,' Shai said, 'told me to always have a backup plan. I couldn't be certain the scepter would even be on display.'

'Ah ...' Frava said. She adopted an almost maternal expression, though it was laden with loathing – hidden poorly – and condescension. 'You requested arbiter intervention in your execution, as most prisoners do. I decided on a whim to agree to your request because I was curious why you had created this painting.' She shook her head. 'But child, you can't honestly believe we'd let you free. With sins like this? You are in a monumentally bad predicament, and our mercy can only be extended so far ...'

Shai glanced toward the other arbiters. The ones seated near the fireplace seemed to be paying no heed, but they did not speak to one another. They were listening. *Something is wrong*, Shai thought. *They're worried.*

Gaotona still stood just to the side. He inspected Shai with eyes that betrayed no emotion.

Frava's manner had the air of one scolding a small child. The lingering end of her comment was intended to make Shai hope for release. Together, that was meant to make her pliable, willing to agree to anything in the hope that she'd be freed.

An opportunity indeed ...

It was time to take control of this conversation.

'You want something from me,' Shai said. 'I'm ready to discuss my payment.'

'Your *payment?*' Frava asked. 'Girl, you are to be executed on the morrow! If we did wish something of you, the payment would be your life.'

'My life is my own,' Shai said. 'And it has been for days now.'

'Please,' Frava said. 'You were locked in the Forger's cell, with thirty different kinds of stone in the wall.'

'Forty-four kinds, actually.'

Gaotona raised an appreciative eyebrow.

Nights! I'm glad I got that right . . .

Shai glanced at Gaotona. 'You thought I wouldn't recognize the grindstone, didn't you? Please. I'm a Forger. I learned stone classification during my first year of training. That block was obviously from the Laio quarry.'

Frava opened her mouth to speak, a slight smile to her lips.

'Yes, I know about the plates of ralkalest, the unForgeable metal, hidden behind the rock wall of my cell,' Shai guessed. 'The wall was a puzzle, meant to distract me. You wouldn't *actually* make a cell out of rocks like limestone, just in case a prisoner gave up on Forgery and tried to chip their way free. You built the wall, but secured it with a plate of ralkalest at the back to cut off escape.'

Frava snapped her mouth shut.

'The problem with ralkalest,' Shai said, 'is that it's not a very strong metal. Oh, the grate at the top of my cell was solid enough, and I couldn't have gotten through that. But a thin plate? Really. Have you heard of anthracite?'

Frava frowned.

'It is a rock that burns,' Gaotona said.

'You gave me a candle,' Shai said, reaching into the small of her back. She tossed her makeshift wooden soulstamp onto the desk. 'All I had to do was Forge the wall and persuade the stones that they're anthracite – not a difficult task, once I knew the forty-four types of rock. I could burn them, and they'd melt that plate behind the wall.'

Shai pulled over a chair, seating herself before the desk. She leaned back. Behind her, the captain of the Strikers growled softly, but Frava drew her lips to a line and said nothing. Shai let her muscles relax, and she breathed a quiet prayer to the Unknown God.

Nights! It looked like they'd actually bought it. She'd worried they'd know enough of Forgery to see through her lie.

'I was going to escape tonight,' Shai said, 'but whatever it is you want me to do must be important, as you're willing to involve a miscreant like myself. And so we come to my payment.'

'I could still have you executed,' Frava said. 'Right now. Here.'

'But you won't, will you?'

Frava set her jaw.

'I warned you that she would be difficult to manipulate,' Gaotona said to Frava. Shai could tell she'd impressed him, but at the same time, his eyes seemed . . . sorrowful? Was that the right emotion? She found this aged man as difficult to read as a book in Svordish.

Frava raised a finger, then swiped it to the side. A servant approached with a small, cloth-wrapped box. Shai's heart leaped upon seeing it.

The man clicked the latches open on the front and raised the top. The case was lined with soft cloth and inset with five depressions made to hold soulstamps. Each cylindrical stone stamp was as long as a finger and as wide as a large man's thumb. The leatherbound notebook set in the case atop them was worn by long use; Shai breathed in a hint of its familiar scent.

They were called Essence Marks, the most powerful kind of soulstamp. Each Essence Mark had to be attuned to a specific individual, and was intended to rewrite their history, personality, and soul for a short time. These five were attuned to Shai.

'Five stamps to rewrite a soul,' Frava said. 'Each is an abomination, illegal to possess. These Essence Marks were to be destroyed this afternoon. Even if you had escaped, you'd have lost these. How long does it take to create one?'

'Years,' Shai whispered.

There were no other copies. Notes and diagrams were too dangerous to leave, even in secret, as such things gave others too much insight to one's soul. She never let these Essence Marks out of her sight, except on the rare occasion they were taken from her.

'You will accept these as payment?' Frava asked, lips turned down, as if discussing a meal of slime and rotted meat.

'Yes.'

Frava nodded, and the servant snapped the case closed. 'Then let me show you what you are to do.'

SHAI HAD NEVER met an emperor before, let alone poked one in the face.

Emperor Ashravan of the Eighty Suns – forty-ninth ruler of the Rose Empire – did not respond as Shai prodded him. He stared ahead blankly, his round cheeks rosy and hale, but his expression completely lifeless.

'What happened?' Shai asked, straightening from beside the emperor's bed. It was in the style of the ancient Lamio people, with a headboard shaped like a phoenix rising toward heaven. She'd seen a sketch of such a headboard in a book; likely the Forgery had been drawn from that source.

'Assassins,' Arbiter Gaotona said. He stood on the other side of the bed, alongside two surgeons. Of the Strikers, only their captain – Zu – had been allowed to enter. 'The murderers broke in two nights ago, attacking the emperor and his wife. She was slain. The emperor received a crossbow bolt to the head.'

'That considered,' Shai noted, 'he's looking remarkable.'

'You are familiar with resealing?' Gaotona asked.

'Vaguely,' Shai said. Her people called it Flesh Forgery. Using it, a surgeon of great skill could Forge a body to remove its wounds and scars. It required great specialization. The Forger had to know each and every sinew, each vein and muscle, in order to accurately heal.

Resealing was one of the few branches of Forgery that Shai hadn't studied in depth. Get an ordinary forgery wrong, and you created a work of poor artistic merit. Get a Flesh Forgery wrong, and people died.

'Our resealers are the best in the world,' Frava said, walking around the foot of the bed, hands behind her back. 'The emperor was attended to quickly following the assassination attempt. The wound to his head was healed, but ...'

'But his mind was not?' Shai asked, waving her hand in front of the man's face again. 'It doesn't sound like they did a very good job at all.'

One of the surgeons cleared his throat. The diminutive man had ears like window shutters that had been thrown open wide on a sunny day. 'Resealing repairs a body and makes it anew. That, however, is much like rebinding a book with fresh paper following a fire. Yes, it may look exactly the same, and it may be whole all the way through. The words, though ... the words are gone. We have given the emperor a new brain. It is merely empty.'

'Huh,' Shai said. 'Did you find out who tried to kill him?'

The five arbiters exchanged glances. Yes, they knew.

'We are not certain,' Gaotona said.

'Meaning,' Shai added, 'you know, but you couldn't prove it well enough to make an accusation. One of the other factions in court, then?'

Gaotona sighed. 'The Glory Faction.'

Shai whistled softly, but it *did* make sense. If the emperor died, there was a good chance that the Glory Faction would win a bid to elevate his successor. At forty, Emperor Ashravan was young still, by Grand standards. He had been expected to rule another fifty years.

If he were replaced, the five arbiters in this room would lose their positions – which, by imperial politics, would be a huge blow to their status. They'd drop from being the most powerful people in the world to being among the lowest of the empire's eighty factions.

'The assassins did not survive their attack,' Frava said. 'The Glory Faction does not yet know whether their ploy succeeded. You are going to replace the emperor's soul with . . .' She took a deep breath. 'With a Forgery.'

They're crazy, Shai thought. Forging one's own soul was difficult enough, and you didn't have to rebuild it from the ground up.

The arbiters had no idea what they were asking. But of course they didn't. They hated Forgery, or so they claimed. They walked on imitation floor tiles past copies of ancient vases, they let their surgeons repair a body, but they didn't call any of these things 'Forgery' in their own tongue.

The Forgery of the soul, that was what they considered an abomination. Which meant Shai really was their only choice. No one in their own government would be capable of this. She probably wasn't either.

'Can you do it?' Gaotona asked.

I have no idea, Shai thought. 'Yes,' she said.

'It will need to be an exact Forgery,' Frava said sternly. 'If the Glory Faction has any inkling of what we've done, they will pounce. The emperor must not act erratically.'

'I said I could do it,' Shai replied. 'But it will be difficult. I will need information about Ashravan and his life, everything we can get. Official histories will be a start, but they'll be too sterile. I will need extensive interviews and writings about him from those who knew him best. Servants, friends, family members. Did he have a journal?'

'Yes,' Gaotona said.

'Excellent.'

'Those documents are sealed,' said one of the other arbiters. 'He wanted them destroyed . . .'

Everyone in the room looked toward the man. He swallowed, then looked down.

'You shall have everything you request,' Frava said.

'I'll need a test subject as well,' Shai said. 'Someone to test my Forgeries on. A Grand, male, someone who was around the emperor a lot and who knew him. That will let me see if I have the personality right.' Nights! Getting the personality right would be secondary. Getting a stamp that actually took . . . that would be the first step. She wasn't certain she could manage even that much. 'And I'll need soulstone, of course.'

Frava regarded Shai, arms folded.

'You can't possibly expect me to do this without soulstone,' Shai said drily. 'I could carve a stamp out of wood, if I had to, but your goal will be difficult enough as it is. Soulstone. Lots of it.'

'Fine,' Frava said. 'But you will be watched these three months. Closely.'

'Three *months*?' Shai said. 'I'm planning for this to take at least two years.'

'You have a hundred days,' Frava said. 'Actually, ninety-eight, now.'

Impossible.

'The official explanation for why the emperor hasn't been seen these last two days,' said one of the other arbiters, 'is that he's been in mourning for the death of his wife. The Glory Faction will assume we are scrambling to buy time following the emperor's death. Once the hundred days of isolation are finished, they will demand that Ashravan present himself to the court. If he does not, we are finished.'

And so are you, the woman's tone implied.

'I will need gold for this,' Shai said. 'Take what you're thinking I'll demand and double it. I will walk out of this country rich.'

'Done,' Frava said.

Too easy, Shai thought. Delightful. They were planning to kill her once this was done.

Well, that gave her ninety-eight days to find a way out. 'Get me those records,' she said. 'I'll need a place to work, plenty of supplies, and my things back.' She held up a finger before they could complain. 'Not my Essence Marks, but everything else. I'm not going to work for three months in the same clothing I've been wearing while in prison. And, as I consider it, have someone draw me a bath immediately.'

DAY THREE

THE NEXT DAY – bathed, well fed, and well rested for the first time since her capture – Shai received a knock at her door.

They'd given her a room. It was tiny, probably the most drab in the entire palace, and it smelled faintly of mildew. They had still posted guards to watch her all night, of course, and – from her memory of the layout of the vast palace – she was in one of the least frequented wings, one used mostly for storage.

Still, it was better than a cell. Barely.

At the knock, Shai looked up from her inspection of the room's old cedar table. It probably hadn't seen an oiling cloth in longer than Shai had been alive. One of her guards opened the door, letting in the elderly Arbiter Gaotona. He carried a box two handspans wide and a couple of inches deep.

Shai rushed over, drawing a glare from Captain Zu, who stood beside the arbiter. 'Keep your distance from his grace,' Zu growled.

'Or what?' Shai asked, taking the box. 'You'll stab me?'

'Someday, I will enjoy—'

'Yes, yes,' Shai said, walking back to her table and flipping open the box's lid. Inside were eighteen soul-stamps, their heads smooth and unetched. She felt a thrill and picked one up, holding it out and inspecting it.

She had her spectacles back now, so no more squinting. She also wore clothing far more fitting than that dingy dress. A flat, red, calf-length skirt and buttoned blouse. The Grands would consider it unfashionable, as among them, ancient-looking robes or wraps were the current style. Shai found those dreary. Under the blouse she wore a tight cotton shirt, and under the skirt she wore leggings. A lady never knew when she might need to ditch her outer layer of clothing to effect a disguise.

'This is good stone,' Shai said of the stamp in her fingers. She took out one of her chisels, which had a tip almost as fine as a pinhead, and began to scrape at the rock. It *was* good soulstone. The rock came away easily and precisely. Soulstone was almost as soft as chalk, but did not chip when scraped. You could carve it with high precision, and then set it with a flame and a mark on the top, which would harden it to a strengthcloser to quartz. The only way to get a better stamp was to carve one from crystal itself, which was incredibly difficult.

For ink, they had provided bright red squid's ink, mixed with a small percentage of wax. Any fresh organic ink would work, though inks from animals were better than inks from plants.

'Did you ... steal a vase from the hallway outside?' Gaotona asked, frowning toward an object sitting at the side of her small room. She'd snatched one of the vases on the way back from the bath. One of her guards had tried to interfere, but Shai had talked her way past the objection. That guard was now blushing.

'I was curious about the skills of your Forgers,' Shai said, setting down her tools and hauling the vase up onto the table. She turned it on its side, showing the bottom and the red seal imprinted into the clay there.

A Forger's seal was easy to spot. It didn't just imprint onto the object's surface, it actually sank *into* the material, creating a depressed pattern of red troughs. The rim of the round seal was red as well, but raised, like an embossing.

You could tell a lot about a person from the way they designed their seals. This one, for example, had a sterile feel to it. No real art, which was a contrast to the minutely detailed and delicate beauty of the vase itself. Shai had heard that the Heritage Faction kept lines of half-trained Forgers working by rote, creating these pieces like rows of men making shoes in a factory.

'Our workers are *not* Forgers,' Gaotona said. 'We don't use that word. They are Rememberers.'

'It's the same thing.'

'They don't touch souls,' Gaotona said sternly. 'Beyond that, what we do is in appreciation of the past, rather than with the aim of fooling or scamming people. Our reminders bring people to a greater understanding of their heritage.'

Shai raised an eyebrow. She took her mallet and chisel, then brought them down at an angle on the embossed rim of the vase's seal. The seal resisted – there was a *force* to it, trying to stay in place – but the blow broke through. The rest of the seal popped up, troughs vanishing, the seal becoming simple ink and losing its powers.

The colors of the vase faded immediately, bleeding to plain grey, and its shape warped. A soulstamp didn't just make visual changes, but rewrote an object's history. Without the stamp, the vase was a horrid piece. Whoever had thrown it hadn't cared about the end product. Perhaps they'd known it would be part of a Forgery. Shai shook her head and turned back to her work on the unfinished soulstamp. This wasn't for the emperor – she wasn't nearly ready for that yet – but carving helped her think.

Gaotona gestured for the guards to leave, all but Zu, who remained by his side. 'You present a puzzle, Forger,' Gaotona said once the other two guards were gone, the door closed. He settled down in one of the two rickety wooden chairs. They – along with the splintery bed, the ancient table, and the trunk with her things – made up the room's entire array of furniture. The single window had a warped frame that let in the breeze, and even the walls had cracks in them.

'A puzzle?' Shai asked, holding up the stamp before her, peering closely at her work. 'What kind of puzzle?'

'You are a Forger. Therefore, you cannot be trusted without supervision. You will try to run the moment you think of a practicable escape.'

'So leave guards with me,' Shai said, carving some more.

'Pardon,' Gaotona said, 'but I doubt it would take you long to bully, bribe, or blackmail them.'

Nearby, Zu stiffened.

'I meant no offense, Captain,' Gaotona said. 'I have great confidence in your people, but what we have before us is a master trickster, liar, and thief. Your best guards would eventually become clay in her hands.'

'Thank you,' Shai said.

'It was *not* a compliment. What your type touches, it corrupts. I worried about leaving you alone even for one day under the supervision of mortal eyes. From what I know of you, you could nearly charm the gods themselves.'

She continued working.

'I cannot trust in manacles to hold you,' Gaotona said softly, 'as we are required to give you soulstone so that you can work on our ... problem. You would turn your manacles to soap, then escape in the night laughing.'

That statement, of course, betrayed a complete lack of understanding in how Forgery worked. A Forgery had to be likely – believable – otherwise it wouldn't take. Who would make a chain out of soap? It would be ridiculous.

What she *could* do, however, was discover the chain's origins and composition, then rewrite one or the other. She could Forge the chain's past so that one of the links had been cast incorrectly, which would give her a flaw to exploit. Even if she could not find the chain's exact history, she might be able to escape – an imperfect stamp would not take for long, but she'd only need a few moments to shatter the link with a mallet.

They could make a chain out of ralkalest, the unForgeable metal, but that would only delay her escape. With enough time, and soulstone, she would find a solution. Forging the wall to have a weak crack in it, so she could pull the chain free. Forging the ceiling to have a loose block, which she could let drop and shatter the weak ralkalest links.

She didn't want to do something so extreme if she didn't have to. 'I don't see that you need to worry about me,' Shai said, still working. 'I am intrigued by what we are doing, and I've been promised wealth. That is enough to keep me here. Don't forget, I could have escaped my previous cell at any time.'

'Ah yes,' Gaotona said. 'The cell in which you would have used Forgery to get through the wall. Tell me, out of curiosity, have you studied anthracite? That rock you said you'd turn the wall into? I seem to recall that it is very difficult to make burn.'

This one is more clever than people give him credit for being.

A candle's flame would have trouble igniting anthracite – on paper, the rock burned at the correct temperature, but getting an entire sample hot enough was very difficult. 'I was fully capable of creating a proper kindling environment with some wood from my bunk and a few rocks turned into coal.'

'Without a kiln?' Gaotona said, sounding faintly amused. 'With no bellows? But that is beside the point. Tell me, how were you planning to *survive* inside a cell where the wall was aflame at over two thousand degrees? Would not that kind of fire suck away all of the breathable air? Ah, but of course. You could have used your bed linens and transformed them into a poor conductor, perhaps glass, and made a shell for yourself to hide in.'

Shai continued her carving, uncomfortable. The way he said that ... Yes, he knew that she could not have done what he described. Most Grands were ignorant about the ways of Forgery, and this man certainly still was, but he *did* know enough to realize she couldn't have escaped as she said. No more than bed linens could become glass.

Beyond that, making the entire wall into another type of rock would have been difficult. She would have had to change too many things – rewritten history so that the quarries for each type of stone were near deposits of anthracite, and that in each case, a block of the burnable rock was quarried by mistake. That was a huge stretch, an almost impossible one, particularly without specific knowledge of the quarries in question.

Plausibility was key to any forgery, magical or not. People

whispered of Forgers turning lead into gold, never realizing that the reverse was far, far easier. Inventing a history for a bar of gold where somewhere along the line, someone had adulterated it with lead … well, that was a plausible lie. The reverse would be so unlikely that a stamp to make that transformation would not take for long.

'You impress me, your grace,' Shai finally said. 'You think like a Forger.'

Gaotona's expression soured.

'That,' she noted, '*was* meant as a compliment.'

'I value truth, young woman. Not Forgery.' He regarded her with the expression of a disappointed grandfather. 'I have seen the work of your hands. That copied painting you did … it was *remarkable*. Yet it was accomplished in the name of lies. What great works could you create if you focused on industry and beauty instead of wealth and deception?'

'What I do *is* great art.'

'No. You copy other people's great art. What you do is technically marvelous, yet completely lacking in spirit.'

She almost slipped in her carving, hands growing tense. How *dare* he? Threatening to execute her was one thing, but insulting her art? He made her sound like … like one of those assembly line Forgers, churning out vase after vase!

She calmed herself with difficulty, then plastered on a smile. Her aunt Sol had once told Shai to smile at the worst insults and snap at the minor ones. That way, no man would know your heart.

'So how *am* I to be kept in line?' she asked. 'We have established that I am among the most vile wretches to slither through the halls of this palace. You cannot bind me and you cannot trust your own soldiers to guard me.'

'Well,' Gaotona said, 'whenever possible, I personally will observe your work.'

She would have preferred Frava – that one seemed as if she'd be easier to manipulate – but this was workable. 'If you wish,' Shai said. 'Much of it will be boring to one who does not understand Forgery.'

'I am not interested in being entertained,' Gaotona said, waving one hand to Captain Zu. 'Whenever I am here, Captain Zu will guard me. He is the only one of our Strikers to know the extent of the emperor's injury, and only he knows of our plan with you. Other guards will watch you during the rest of the day, and you are *not* to speak to them of your task. There will be no rumors of what we do.'

'You don't need to worry about me talking,' Shai said, truthfully for once. 'The more people who know of a Forgery, the more likely it is to fail.' *Besides*, she thought, *if I told the guards, you'd undoubtedly execute them to preserve your secrets.* She didn't like Strikers, but she liked the empire less, and the guards were really just another kind of slave. Shai wasn't in the business of getting people killed for no reason.

'Excellent,' Gaotona said. 'The second method of insuring your … attention to your project waits outside. If you would, good Captain?'

Zu opened the door. A cloaked figure stood with the guards. The figure stepped into the room; his walk was lithe, but somehow unnatural. After Zu closed the door, the figure removed his hood, revealing a face with milky white skin and red eyes.

Shai hissed softly through her teeth. 'And you call what *I* do an abomination?'

Gaotona ignored her, standing up from his chair to regard the newcomer. 'Tell her.'

The newcomer rested long white fingers on her door, inspecting it. 'I will place the rune here,' he said in an accented voice. 'If she leaves this room for any reason, or if she alters the rune or the door, I will know. My pets will come for her.'

Shai shivered. She glared at Gaotona. 'A Bloodsealer. You invited a *Bloodsealer* into your palace?'

'This one has proven himself an asset recently,' Gaotona said. 'He is loyal and he is discreet. He is also very effective. There are ... times when one must accept the aid of darkness in order to contain a greater darkness.'

Shai hissed softly as the Bloodsealer removed something from within his robes. A crude soulstamp created from a bone. His 'pets' would also be bone, Forgeries of human life crafted from the skeletons of the dead.

The Bloodsealer looked to her.

Shai backed away. 'Surely you don't expect—'

Zu took her by the arms. Nights, but he was strong. She panicked. Her Essence Marks! She needed her Essence Marks! With those, she could fight, escape, run ...

Zu cut her along the back of her arm. She barely felt the shallow wound, but she struggled anyway. The Bloodsealer stepped up and inked his horrid tool in Shai's blood. He then turned and pressed the stamp against the center of her door.

When he withdrew his hand, he left a glowing red seal in the wood. It was shaped like an eye. The moment he marked the seal, Shai felt a sharp pain in her arm, where she'd been cut.

Shai gasped, eyes wide. Never had any person *dared* do such a thing to her. Almost better that she had been executed! Almost better that—

Control yourself, she told herself forcibly. *Become someone who can deal with this.*

She took a deep breath and let herself become someone else. An imitation of herself who was calm, even in a situation like this. It was a crude forgery, just a trick of the mind, but it worked.

She shook herself free from Zu, then accepted the kerchief Gaotona handed her. She glared at the Bloodsealer as the pain in her arm faded. He smiled at her with lips that were white and faintly translucent, like the skin of a maggot. He nodded to Gaotona before replacing his hood and stepping out of the room, closing the door after.

Shai forced herself to breathe evenly, calming herself. There was no subtlety to what the Bloodsealer did; they didn't traffic in subtlety. Instead of skill or artistry, they used tricks and blood. However, their craft was effective. The man would know if Shai left the room, and he had her fresh blood on his stamp, which was attuned to her. With that, his undead pets would be able to hunt her no matter where she ran.

Gaotona settled back down in his chair. 'You know what will happen if you flee?'

Shai glared at Gaotona.

'You now realize how desperate we are,' he said softly, lacing his fingers before him. 'If you do run, we will give you to the Bloodsealer. Your bones will become his next pet. This promise was all he requested in payment. You may begin your work, Forger. Do it well, and you will escape this fate.'

DAY FIVE

WORK SHE DID.

Shai began digging through accounts of the emperor's life. Few people understood how much Forgery was about study and research. It was an art any man or woman could learn; it required only a steady hand and an eye for detail.

That and a willingness to spend weeks, months, even *years* preparing the ideal soulstamp.

Shai didn't have years. She felt rushed as she read biography after biography, often staying up well into the night taking notes. She did not believe that she could do what they asked of her. Creating a believable Forgery of another man's soul, particularly in such a short time, just wasn't possible. Unfortunately, she had to make a good show of it while she planned her escape.

They didn't let her leave the room. She used a chamber pot when nature called, and for baths she was allowed a tub of warm water and cloths. She was under supervision at all times, even when bathing.

That Bloodsealer came each morning to renew his mark on the door. Each time, the act required a little blood from Shai. Her arms were soon laced with shallow cuts.

All the while, Gaotona visited. The ancient arbiter studied

her as she read, watching with those eyes that judged … but also did not hate.

As she formulated her plans, she decided one thing: getting free would probably require manipulating this man in some way.

DAY TWELVE

SHAI PRESSED HER stamp down on the tabletop.

As always, the stamp sank slightly into the material. A soulstamp left a seal you could feel, regardless of the material. She twisted the stamp a half turn – this did not blur the ink, though she did not know why. One of her mentors had taught that it was because by this point the seal was touching the object's soul and not its physical presence.

When she pulled the stamp back, it left a bright red seal in the wood as if carved there. Transformation sprcad from the scal in a wave. The table's dull grey splintery cedar became beautiful and well maintained, with a warm patina that reflected the light of the candles sitting across from her.

Shai rested her fingers on the new table; it was now smooth to the touch. The sides and legs were finely carved, inlaid here and there with silver.

Gaotona sat upright, lowering the book he'd been reading. Zu shuffled in discomfort at seeing the Forgery.

'What was that?' Gaotona demanded.

'I was tired of getting splinters,' Shai said, settling back in her chair. It creaked. *You are next*, she thought.

Gaotona stood up and walked to the table. He touched it, as if expecting the transformation to be mere illusion. It was not. The fine table now looked horribly out of place in the dingy room. 'This is what you've been doing?'

'Carving helps me think.'

'You should be focused on your task!' Gaotona said. 'This is frivolity. The empire itself is in danger!'

No, Shai thought. *Not the empire itself; just your rule of it.* Unfortunately, after eleven days, she still didn't have an angle on Gaotona, not one she could exploit.

'I *am* working on your problem, Gaotona,' she said. 'What you ask of me is hardly a simple task.'

'And changing that table was?'

'Of course it was,' Shai said. 'All I had to do was rewrite its past so that it was maintained, rather than being allowed to sink into disrepair. That took hardly any work at all.'

Gaotona hesitated, then knelt beside the table. 'These carvings, this inlay ... those were not part of the original.'

'I might have added a little.'

She wasn't certain if the Forgery would take or not. In a few minutes, that seal might evaporate and the table might revert to its previous state. Still, she was fairly certain she'd guessed the table's past well enough. Some of the histories she was reading mentioned what gifts had come from where. This table, she suspected, had come from far-off Svorden as a gift to Emperor Ashravan's predecessor. The strained relationship with Svorden had then led the emperor to lock it away and ignore it.

'I don't recognize this piece,' Gaotona said, still looking at the table.

'Why should you?'

'I have studied ancient arts extensively,' he said. 'This is from the Vivare dynasty?'

'No.'

'An imitation of the work of Chamrav?'

'No.'

'What then?'

'Nothing,' Shai said with exasperation. 'It's not imitating anything; it has become a better version of itself.' That was a maxim of good Forgery: improve slightly on an original, and people would often accept the fake because it *was* superior.

Gaotona stood up, looking troubled. *He's thinking again that my talent is wasted*, Shai thought with annoyance, moving aside a stack of accounts of the emperor's life. Collected at her request, these came from palace servants. She didn't want only the official histories. She needed authenticity, not sterilized recitations.

Gaotona stepped back to his chair. 'I do not see how transforming this table could have taken hardly any work, although it clearly must be much simpler than what you have been asked to do. Both seem incredible to me.'

'Changing a human soul is far more difficult.'

'I can accept that conceptually, but I do not know the specifics. Why is it so?'

She glanced at him. *He wants to know more of what I'm doing*, she thought, *so that he can tell how I'm preparing to escape.* He knew she would be trying, of course. They both would pretend that neither knew that fact.

'All right,' she said, standing and walking to the wall of her room. 'Let's talk about Forgery. Your cage for me had a wall of forty-four types of stone, mostly as a trap to keep me distracted. I had to figure out the makeup and origin of each block if I wanted to try to escape. Why?'

'So you could create a Forgery of the wall, obviously.'

'But why all of them?' she asked. 'Why not just change one block or a few? Why not just make a hole big enough to slip into, creating a tunnel for myself?'

'I . . .' He frowned. 'I have no idea.'

Shai rested her hand against the outer wall of her room. It had been painted, though the paint was coming off in several sections. She could feel the separate stones. 'All things exist in three Realms, Gaotona. Physical, Cognitive, Spiritual. The Physical is what we feel, what is before us. The Cognitive is how an object is viewed and how it views itself. The Spiritual Realm contains an object's soul – its essence – as well as the ways it is connected to the things and people around it.'

'You must understand,' Gaotona said, 'I don't subscribe to your pagan superstitions.'

'Yes, you worship the sun instead,' Shai said, failing to keep the amusement out of her voice. 'Or, rather, eighty suns – believing that even though each looks the same, a different sun actually rises each day. Well, you wanted to know how Forgery works, and why the emperor's soul will be so difficult to reproduce. The Realms are important to this.'

'Very well.'

'Here is the point. The longer an object exists as a whole, and the longer it is *seen* in that state, the stronger its sense of complete identity becomes. That table is made up of various pieces of wood fitted together, but do we think of it that way? No. We see the whole.

'To Forge the table, I must understand it as a whole. The same goes for a wall. That wall has existed long enough to view itself as a single entity. I could, perhaps, have attacked each block separately – they might still be distinct enough – but doing so would be difficult, as the wall wants to act as a whole.'

'The wall,' Gaotona said flatly, '*wants* to be treated as a whole.'

'Yes.'

'You imply that the wall has a soul.'

'All things do,' she said. 'Each object sees itself as something. Connection and intent are vital. This is why, master Arbiter, I can't simply write down a personality for your emperor, stamp him, and be done. Seven reports I've read say his favorite color was green. Do you know why?'

'No,' Gaotona said. 'Do you?'

'I'm not sure yet,' Shai said. 'I *think* it was because his brother, who died when Ashravan was six, had always been fond of it. The emperor latched on to it, as it reminds him of his dead sibling. There might be a touch of nationalism to it as well, as he was born in Ukurgi, where the provincial flag is predominantly green.'

Gaotona seemed troubled. 'You must know something that specific?'

'Nights, yes! And a thousand things just as detailed. I can get some wrong. I *will* get some wrong. Most of them, hopefully, won't matter – they will make his personality a little off, but each person changes day to day in any case. If I get too many wrong, though, the personality won't matter because the stamp won't take. At least, it won't last long enough to do any good. I assume that if your emperor has to be restamped every fifteen minutes, the charade will be impossible to maintain.'

'You assume correctly.'

Shai sat down with a sigh, looking over her notes.

'You said you could do this,' Gaotona said.

'Yes.'

'You've done it before, with your own soul.'

'I know my own soul,' she said. 'I know my own history. I know what I can change to get the effect I need – and even getting my own Essence Marks right was difficult. Now I not only have to do this for another person, but the transformation must be far more extensive. And I have ninety days left to do it.'

Gaotona nodded slowly.

'Now,' she said, 'you should tell me what you're doing to keep up the pretense that the emperor is still awake and well.'

'We're doing all that needs to be done.'

'I'm far from confident that you are. I think you'll find me a fair bit better at deception than most.'

'I think that *you* will be surprised,' Gaotona said. 'We are, after all, politicians.'

'All right, fine. But you are sending food, aren't you?'

'Of course,' Gaotona said. 'Three meals are sent to the emperor's quarters each day. They return to the palace kitchens eaten, though he is, of course, secretly being fed broth. He drinks it when prompted, but stares ahead, as if both deaf and mute.'

'And the chamber pot?'

'He has no control over himself,' Gaotona said, grimacing. 'We keep him in cloth diapers.'

'Nights, man! And no one changes a fake chamber pot? Don't you think that's suspicious? Maids will gossip, as will guards at the door. You need to consider these things!'

Gaotona had the decency to blush. 'I will see that it happens, though I don't like the idea of someone else entering his quarters. Too many have a chance to discover what has happened to him.'

'Pick someone you trust, then,' Shai said. 'In fact, make a

rule at the emperor's doors. No one enters unless they bear a card with your personal signet. And yes, I know why you are opening your mouth to object. I know exactly how well guarded the emperor's quarters are – that was part of what I studied to break into the gallery. Your security isn't tight enough, as the assassins proved. Do what I suggest. The more layers of security, the better. If what has happened to the emperor gets out, I have no doubt that I'll end up back in that cell waiting for execution.'

Gaotona sighed, but nodded. 'What else do you suggest?'

DAY SEVENTEEN

A COOL BREEZE laden with unfamiliar spices crept through the cracks around Shai's warped window. The low hum of cheers seeped through as well. Outside, the city celebrated. Delbahad, a holiday no one had known about until two years earlier. The Heritage Faction continued to dig up and revive ancient feasts in an effort to sway public opinion back toward them.

It wouldn't help. The empire was not a republic, and the only ones who would have a say in anointing a new emperor would be the arbiters of the various factions. Shai turned her attention away from the celebrations, and continued to read from the emperor's journal.

I have decided, at long last, to agree to the demands of my faction, the book read. *I will offer myself for the position of emperor, as Gaotona has so often encouraged. Emperor Yazad grows weak with his disease, and a new choice will be made soon.*

Shai made a notation. Gaotona had encouraged Ashravan to seek the throne. And yet, later in the journal, Ashravan spoke of Gaotona with contempt. Why the change? She finished the notation, then turned to another entry years later.

Emperor Ashravan's personal journal fascinated her. He had written it with his own hand, and had included instructions for it to be destroyed upon his death. The arbiters had delivered the journal to her reluctantly, and with vociferous justification. He hadn't died. His body still lived. Therefore, it was just fine for them *not* to burn his writings.

They spoke with confidence, but she could see the uncertainty in their eyes. They were easy to read – all but Gaotona, whose inner thoughts continued to elude her. They didn't understand the purpose of this journal. Why write, they wondered, if not for posterity? Why put your thoughts to paper if not for the purpose of having others read them?

As easy, she thought, *to ask a Forger why she would get satisfaction from creating a fake and seeing it on display without a single person knowing it was her work – and not that of the original artist – they were revering.*

The journal told her far more about the emperor than the official histories had, and not just because of the contents. The pages of the book were worn and stained from constant turning. Ashravan *had* written this book to be read – by himself.

What memories had Ashravan sought so profoundly that he would read this book over and over and over again? Was he vain, enjoying the thrill of past conquests? Was he, instead, insecure? Did he spend hours searching these words because he wanted to justify his mistakes? Or was there another reason?

The door to her chambers opened. They had stopped knocking. Why would they? They already denied her any semblance of privacy. She was still a captive, just a more important one than before.

Arbiter Frava entered, graceful and long faced, wearing robes of a soft violet. Her grey braid was spun with gold and violet this time. Captain Zu guarded her. Inwardly, Shai sighed, adjusting her spectacles. She had been anticipating a night of study and planning, uninterrupted now that Gaotona had gone to join the festivities.

'I am told,' Frava said, 'that you are progressing at an unremarkable pace.'

Shai set down the book. 'Actually, this is quick. I am nearly ready to begin crafting stamps. As I reminded Arbiter Gaotona earlier today, I do still need a test subject who knew the emperor. The connection between them will allow me to test stamps on him, and they will stick briefly – long enough for me to try out a few things.'

'One will be provided,' Frava replied, walking along the table with its glistening surface. She ran a finger across it, then stopped at the red seal mark. The arbiter prodded at it. 'Such an eyesore. After going to such trouble to make the table more beautiful, why not put the seal on the bottom?'

'I'm proud of my work,' Shai said. 'Any Forger who sees this can inspect it and see what I've done.'

Frava sniffed. 'You should not be proud of something like this, little thief. Besides, isn't the point of what you do to *hide* the fact that you've done it?'

'Sometimes,' Shai said. 'When I imitate a signature or counterfeit a painting, the subterfuge is part of the act. But with Forgery, true Forgery, you cannot hide what you've done. The stamp will always be there, describing exactly what has happened. You might as well be proud of it.'

It was the odd conundrum of her life. To be a Forger was not just about soulstamps – it was about the art of mimicry in its entirety. Writing, art, personal signets … an apprentice Forger – mentored half in secret by her people – learned all mundane forgery before being taught to use soulstamps.

The stamps were the highest order of their art, but they were the most difficult to hide. Yes, a seal could be placed in an out-of-the way place on an object, then covered over. Shai had done that very thing on occasion. However, so long as the seal was somewhere to be found, a Forgery could not be perfect.

'Leave us,' Frava said to Zu and the guards.

'But—' Zu said, stepping forward.

'I do not like to repeat myself, Captain,' Frava said.

Zu growled softly, but bowed in obedience. He gave Shai a glare – that was practically a second occupation for him, these days – and retreated with his men. They shut the door with a click.

The Bloodsealer's stamp still hung there on the door, renewed this morning. The Bloodsealer came at the same time most days. Shai had kept specific notes. On days when he was a little late, his seal started to dim right before he arrived. He always got to her in time to renew it, but perhaps someday …

Frava inspected Shai, eyes calculating.

Shai met that gaze with a steady one of her own. 'Zu assumes I'm going to do something horrible to you while we're alone.'

'Zu is simpleminded,' Frava said, 'though he is very useful when someone needs to be killed. Hopefully you won't ever have to experience his efficiency firsthand.'

'You're not worried?' Shai said. 'You are alone in a room with a monster.'

'I'm alone in a room with an opportunist,' Frava said, strolling to the door and inspecting the seal burning there. 'You won't harm me. You're too curious about why I sent the guards away.'

Actually, Shai thought, *I know precisely why you sent them away. And why you came to me during a time when all of your associate arbiters were guaranteed to be busy at the festival.* She waited for Frava to make the offer.

'Has it occurred to you,' Frava said, 'how ... useful to the empire it would be to have an emperor who listened to a voice of wisdom when it spoke to him?'

'Surely Emperor Ashravan already did that.'

'On occasion,' Frava said. 'On other occasions, he could be ... belligerently foolish. Wouldn't it be amazing if, upon his rebirth, he were found lacking that tendency?'

'I thought you wanted him to act exactly like he used to,' Shai said. 'As close to the real thing as possible.'

'True, true. But you are renowned as one of the greatest Forgers ever to live, and I have it on good authority that you are specifically talented with stamping your own soul. Surely you can replicate dear Ashravan's soul with authenticity, yet also make him inclined to listen to reason ... when that reason is spoken by specific individuals.'

Nights afire, Shai thought. *You're willing to just come out and say it, aren't you? You want me to build a back door into the emperor's soul, and you don't even have the decency to feel ashamed about that.*

'I ... might be able to do such a thing,' Shai said, as if considering it for the first time. 'It would be difficult. I'd need a reward worth the effort.'

'A suitable reward *would* be appropriate,' Frava said, turning to her. 'I realize you were probably planning to leave the Imperial Seat following your release, but why? This city could be a place of great opportunity to you, with a sympathetic ruler on the throne.'

'Be more blunt, Arbiter,' Shai said. 'I have a long night ahead of me studying while others celebrate. I don't have the mind for word games.'

'The city has a thriving clandestine smuggling trade,' Frava said. 'Keeping track of it has been a hobby of mine. It would serve me to have someone proper running it. I will give it to you, should you do this task for me.'

That was always their mistake – assuming they knew why Shai did what she did. Assuming she'd jump at a chance like this, assuming that a smuggler and a Forger were basically the same thing because they both disobeyed someone else's laws.

'That sounds pleasant,' Shai said, smiling her most genuine smile – the one that had an edge of overt deceptiveness to it.

Frava smiled deeply in return. 'I will leave you to consider,' she said, pulling open the door and clapping for the guards to reenter.

Shai sank down into her chair, horrified. Not because of the offer – she'd been expecting one like it for days now – but because she had only now understood the implications. The offer of the smuggling trade was, of course, false. Frava might have been able to deliver such a thing, but she wouldn't. Even assuming that the woman hadn't already been planning to have Shai killed, this offer sealed that eventuality.

There was more to it, though. Far more. *So far as she knows, she just planted in my head the idea of building control into the emperor. She won't trust my Forgery. She'll be expecting me to put in back doors of my own, ones that give* me *and not her complete control over Ashravan.*

What did that mean?

It meant that Frava had another Forger standing by. One, likely, without the talent or the bravado to try Forging someone else's soul – but one who could look over Shai's work and find any back doors she put in. This Forger would be better trusted, and could rewrite Shai's work to put Frava in control.

They might even be able to finish Shai's work, if she got it far enough along first. Shai had intended to use the full hundred days to plan her escape, but now she realized that her sudden extermination could come at any time.

The closer she got to finishing the project, the more likely that grew.

DAY THIRTY

'THIS IS NEW,' Gaotona said, inspecting the stained glass window.

That had been a particularly pleasing bit of inspiration on Shai's part. Attempts to Forge the window to a better version of itself had repeatedly failed; each time, after five minutes or so, the window had reverted to its cracked, gap-sided self.

Then Shai had found a bit of colored glass rammed into one side of the frame. The window, she realized, had once been a stained glass piece, like many in the palace. It had been broken, and whatever had shattered the window had also bent the frame, producing those gaps that let in the frigid breeze.

Rather than repairing it as it had been meant to be, someone had put ordinary glass into the window and left it to crack. A stamp from Shai in the bottom right corner had restored the window, rewriting its history so that a caring master craftsman had discovered the fallen window and remade it. That seal had taken immediately. Even after all this time, the window had seen itself as something beautiful.

Or maybe she was just getting romantic again.

'You said you would bring me a test subject today,' Shai said, blowing the dust off the end of a freshly carved soul-stamp. She engraved a series of quick marks on the back – the side opposite the elaborately carved front. The setting mark finished every soulstamp, indicating no more carving was to come. Shai had always fancied it to look like the shape of MaiPon, her homeland.

Those marks finished, she held the stamp over a flame. This was a property of soulstone; fire hardened it, so it could not be chipped. She didn't need to take this step. The anchoring marks on the top were all it really needed, and she could carve a stamp out of anything, really, so long as the carving was precise. Soulstone was prized, however, because of this hardening process.

Once the entire thing was blackened from the candle's flame – first one end, then the other – she held it up and blew on it strongly. Flakes of char blew free with her breath, revealing the beautiful red and grey marbled stone beneath.

'Yes,' Gaotona said. 'A test subject. I brought one, as promised.' Gaotona crossed the small room toward the door, where Zu stood guard.

Shai leaned back in her chair, which she'd Forged into something far more comfortable a couple of days back, and waited. She had made a bet with herself. Would the subject be one of the emperor's guards? Or would it be some lowly palace functionary, perhaps the man who took notes for Ashravan? Which person would the arbiters force to endure Shai's blasphemy in the name of a supposedly greater good?

Gaotona sat down in the chair by the door.

'Well?' Shai asked.

He raised his hands to the sides. 'You may begin.'

Shai dropped her feet to the ground, sitting up straight. 'You?'

'Yes.'

'You're one of the arbiters! One of the most powerful people in the empire!'

'Ah,' he said. 'I had not noticed. I fit your specifications. I am male, was born in Ashravan's own birthplace, and I knew him very well.'

'But . . .' Shai trailed off.

Gaotona leaned forward, clasping his hands. 'We debated this for weeks. Other options were offered, but it was determined that we could not in good conscience order one of our people to undergo this blasphemy. The only conclusion was to offer up one of ourselves.'

Shai shook herself free of shock. *Frava would have had no trouble ordering someone else to this*, she thought. *Nor would the others. You must have insisted upon this, Gaotona.*

They considered him a rival; they were probably happy to let him fall to Shai's supposedly horrible, twisted acts. What she planned was perfectly harmless, but there was no way she'd convince a Grand of that. Still, she found herself wishing she could put Gaotona at ease as she pulled her chair up beside him and opened the small box of stamps she had crafted over the past three weeks.

'These stamps will not take,' she said, holding up one of them. 'That is a Forger's term for a stamp that makes a change that is too unnatural to be stable. I doubt any of these will affect you for longer than a minute – and that's assuming I did them correctly.'

Gaotona hesitated, then nodded.

'The human soul is different from that of an object,' Shai continued. 'A person is constantly growing, changing, shifting. That makes a soulstamp used on a person wear out in a way that doesn't happen with objects. Even in the best of cases, a soulstamp used on a person lasts only a day. My Essence Marks are an example. After about twenty-six hours, they fade away.'

'So ... the emperor?'

'If I do my job well,' Shai said, 'he will need to be stamped each morning, much as the Bloodsealer stamps my door. I will fashion into the seal, however, the capacity for him to remember, grow, and learn – he won't revert back to the same state each morning, and will be able to build upon the foundation I give him. However, much as a human body wears down and needs sleep, a soulstamp on one of us must be reset. Fortunately, anyone can do the stamping – Ashravan himself should be able to – once the stamp itself is prepared correctly.'

She gave Gaotona the stamp she held, letting him inspect it.

'Each of the particular stamps I will use today,' she continued, 'will change something small about your past or your innate personality. As you are not Ashravan, the changes will not take. However, you two are similar enough in history that the seals should last for a short time, if I've done them well.'

'You mean this is a ... pattern for the emperor's soul?' Gaotona asked, looking over the stamp.

'No. Just a Forgery of a small part of it. I'm not even sure if the final product will work. So far as I know, no one has ever tried something exactly like this before. But there are accounts of people Forging someone else's soul for ... nefarious purposes. I'm drawing on that knowledge to accomplish this. From what I know, if these seals last for at least a minute on you, they should last far longer on the emperor, as they are attuned to his specific past.'

'A small piece of his soul,' Gaotona said, handing back the

seal. 'So these tests ... you will not use these seals in the final product?'

'No, but I'll take the patterns that work and incorporate them into a greater fabrication. Think of these seals as single characters in a large scroll; once I am done, I'll be able to put them together and tell a story. The story of a man's history and personality. Unfortunately, even if the Forgery takes, there will be small differences. I suggest that you begin spreading rumors that the emperor was wounded. Not terribly, mind you, but imply a good knock to the head. That will explain discrepancies.'

'There are already rumors of his death,' Gaotona said, 'spread by the Glory Faction.'

'Well, indicate he was wounded instead.'

'But—'

Shai raised the stamp. 'Even if I accomplish the impossible – which, mind you, I've done only on rare occasions – the Forgery will not have all of the emperor's memories. It can only contain things I have been able to read about or guess. Ashravan will have had many private conversations that the Forgery will *not* be able to recall. I can imbue him with a keen ability to fake – I have a particular understanding of that sort of thing – but fakery can only take a person so far. Eventually, someone will realize that he has large holes in his memory. Spread the rumors, Gaotona. You're going to need them.'

He nodded, then pulled back his sleeve to expose his arm for her to stamp. She raised the stamp, and Gaotona sighed, then squeezed his eyes shut and nodded again.

She pressed it against his skin. As always, when the stamp touched the skin, it felt as if she were pressing it against something rigid – as if his arm had become stone. The stamp *sank in* slightly. That made for a disconcerting sensation when working on a person. She rotated the stamp, then pulled it back, leaving a red seal on Gaotona's arm. She took out her pocket watch, observing the ticking hand.

The seal gave off faint wisps of red smoke; that happened only when living things were stamped. The soul fought against the rewriting. The seal didn't puff away immediately, though. Shai released a held breath. That was a good sign.

She wondered ... if she were to try something like this on the emperor, would his soul fight against the invasion? Or instead, would it accept the stamp, wishing to have righted what had gone wrong? Much as that window had wanted to be restored to its former beauty. She didn't know.

Gaotona opened his eyes. 'Did it ... work?'

'It took, for now,' Shai said.

'I don't feel any different.'

'That is the point. If the emperor could *feel* the stamp's effects, he would realize that something was wrong. Now, answer me without thought; speak by instinct only. What is your favorite color?'

'Green,' he said immediately.

'Why?'

'Because ...' He trailed off, cocking his head. 'Because it is.'

'And your brother?'

'I hardly remember him,' Gaotona said with a shrug. 'He died when I was very young.'

'It is good he did,' Shai said. 'He would have made a terrible emperor, if he had been chosen in—'

Gaotona stood up. 'Don't you dare speak ill of him! I will have you ...' He stiffened, glancing at Zu, who had reached for his sword in alarm. 'I ... Brother ...?'

The seal faded away.

'A minute and five seconds,' Shai said. 'That one looks good.'

Gaotona raised a hand to his head. 'I can remember having a brother. But ... I don't have one, and never have. I can remember idolizing him; I can remember pain when he died. Such *pain* ...'

'That will fade,' Shai said. 'The impressions will wash away like the remnants of a bad dream. In an hour, you'll barely be able to recall what it was that upset you.' She scribbled some notes. 'I think you reacted too strongly to me insulting your brother's memory. Ashravan worshipped his brother, but kept his feelings buried deep out of guilt that perhaps his brother would have made a better emperor than he.'

'What? Are you sure?'

'About this?' Shai said. 'Yes. I'll have to revise that stamp a little bit, but I think it is mostly right.'

Gaotona sat back down, regarding her with ancient eyes that seemed to be trying to pierce her, to dig deep inside. 'You know a great deal about people.'

'It's one of the early steps of our training,' Shai said. 'Before we're even allowed to *touch* soulstone.'

'Such potential ...' Gaotona whispered.

Shai forced down an immediate burst of annoyance. How dare he look at her like that, as if she were wasting her life? She loved Forgery. The thrill, a life spent getting ahead by her wits. That was what she *was*. Wasn't it?

She thought of one specific Essence Mark, locked away with the others. It was one Mark she had never used, yet was at the same time the most precious of the five.

'Let's try another,' Shai said, ignoring those eyes of

Gaotona's. She couldn't afford to grow offended. Aunt Sol had always said that pride would be Shai's greatest danger in life.

'Very well,' Gaotona said, 'but I am confused at one thing. From what little you've told me of this process, I cannot fathom why these seals even begin to work on me. Don't you need to know a thing's history exactly to make a seal work on it?'

'To make them stick, yes,' Shai said. 'As I've said, it's about plausibility.'

'But this is completely implausible! I don't have a brother.'

'Ah. Well, let me see if I can explain,' she said, settling back. 'I am rewriting your soul to match that of the emperor – just as I rewrote the history of that window to include new stained glass. In both cases, it works because of *familiarity*. The window frame knows what a stained glass window should look like. It once had stained glass in it. Even though the new window is not the same as the one it once held, the seal works because the general concept of a stained glass window has been fulfilled.

'You spent a great deal of time around the emperor. Your soul is familiar with his, much as the window frame is familiar with the stained glass. This is why I have to try out the seals on someone like you, and not on myself. When I stamp you, it's like ... it's like I'm presenting to your soul a piece of something it should know. It only works if the piece is very small, but so long as it is – and so long as the soul considers the piece a familiar part of Ashravan, as I've indicated – the stamp will take for a brief time before being rejected.'

Gaotona regarded her with bemusement.

'Sounds like superstitious nonsense to you, I assume?' Shai said.

'It is ... rather mystical,' Gaotona said, spreading his hands before him. 'A window frame knowing the "concept" of a stained glass window? A soul understanding the concept of another soul?'

'These things exist beyond us,' Shai said, preparing another seal. 'We think about windows, we know about windows; what is and isn't a window takes on … meaning, in the Spiritual Realm. Takes on life, after a fashion. Believe the explanation or do not; I guess it doesn't matter. The fact is that I can try these seals on you, and if they stick for at least a minute, it's a very good indication that I've hit on something.

'Ideally, I'd try this on the emperor himself, but in his state, he would not be able to answer my questions. I need to not only get these to take, but I need to make them work together – and that will require your explanations of what you are feeling so I can nudge the design in the right directions. Now, your arm again, please?'

'Very well.' Gaotona composed himself, and Shai pressed another seal against his arm. She locked it with a half turn, but as soon as she pulled the stamp away, the seal vanished in a puff of red.

'Blast,' Shai said.

'What happened?' Gaotona said, reaching fingers to his arm. He smeared mundane ink; the seal had vanished so quickly, the ink hadn't even been incorporated into its workings. 'What have you done to me this time?'

'Nothing, it appears,' Shai said, inspecting the head of the stamp for flaws. She found none. 'I had *that* one wrong. Very wrong.'

'What was it?'

'The reason Ashravan agreed to become emperor,' Shai said. 'Nights afire. I was certain I had this one.' She shook her head, setting the stamp aside. Ashravan, it appeared, had not stepped up to offer himself as emperor because of a deep-seated desire to prove himself to his family and to escape the distant – but long – shadow of his brother.

'I can tell you why he did it, Forger,' Gaotona said.

She eyed him. *This man encouraged Ashravan to step toward the imperial throne*, she thought. Ashravan eventually hated him for it. *I think.*

'All right,' she said. 'Why?'

'He wanted to change things,' Gaotona said. 'In the empire.'

'He doesn't speak of this in his journal.'

'Ashravan was a humble man.'

Shai raised an eyebrow. That didn't match the reports she'd been given.

'Oh, he had a temper,' Gaotona said. 'And if you got him arguing, he would sink his teeth in and hold fast to his point. But the man ... the man he was ... Deep down, that was a humble man. You will have to understand this about him.'

'I see,' she said. *You did it to him too, didn't you?* Shai thought. *That look of disappointment, that implication we should be better people than we are.* Shai wasn't the only one who felt that Gaotona regarded her as if he were a displeased grandfather.

That made her want to dismiss the man as irrelevant. Except ... he had offered himself to her tests. He thought what she did was horrible, so he insisted on taking the punishment himself, instead of sending another.

You're genuine, aren't you, old man? Shai thought as Gaotona sat back, eyes distant as he considered the emperor. She found herself displeased.

In her business, there were many who laughed at honest men, calling them easy pickings. That was a fallacy. Being honest did not make one naive. A dishonest fool and an honest fool were equally easy to scam; you just went about it in different ways.

However, a man who was honest and clever was always, *always* more difficult to scam than someone who was both dishonest and clever.

Sincerity. It was so difficult, by definition, to fake.

'What are you thinking behind those eyes of yours?' Gaotona asked, leaning forward.

'I was thinking that you must have treated the emperor as you did me, annoying him with constant nagging about what he should accomplish.'

Gaotona snorted. 'I probably did just that. It does not mean my points are, or were, incorrect. He could have ... well, he could have become more than he did. Just as you *could* become a marvelous artist.'

'I am one.'

'A real one.'

'I am one.'

Gaotona shook his head. 'Frava's painting ... there is something we are missing about it, isn't there? She had the forgery inspected, and the assessors found a few tiny mistakes. I couldn't see them without help – but they are there. Upon reflection, they seem odd to me. The strokes are impeccable, masterful even. The style is a perfect match. If you could manage that, why would you have made such errors as putting the moon too low? It's a subtle mistake, but it occurs to me that you would never have made such an error – not unintentionally, at least.'

Shai turned to get another seal.

'The painting they think is the original,' Gaotona said, 'the one hanging in Frava's office right now … It's a fake too, isn't it?'

'Yes,' Shai admitted with a sigh. 'I swapped the paintings a few days before trying for the scepter; I was investigating palace security. I sneaked into the gallery, entered Frava's offices, and made the change as a test.'

'So the one they assume is fake, *it* must be the original,' Gaotona said, smiling. 'You painted those mistakes *over* the original to make it seem like it was a replica!'

'Actually, no,' Shai said. 'Though I have used that trick in the past. They're both fakes. One is simply the obvious fake, planted to be discovered in case something went wrong.'

'So the original is still hidden somewhere …' Gaotona said, sounding curious. 'You sneaked into the palace to investigate security, then you replaced the original painting with a copy. You left a second, slightly worse copy in your room as a false trail. If you were found out while sneaking in – or if you were for some reason sold out by an ally – we would search your room and find the poor copy, and assume that you hadn't yet accomplished your swap. The officers would take the good copy and believe it to be authentic. That way, no one would keep looking for the original.'

'More or less.'

'That's very clever,' Gaotona said. 'Why, if you were captured sneaking into the palace trying to steal the scepter, you could confess that you were trying to steal only the painting. A search of your room would turn up the fake, and you'd be charged with attempted theft from an individual, in this case Frava, which is a much lesser crime than trying to steal an imperial relic. You would get ten years of labor instead of a death sentence.'

'Unfortunately,' Shai said, 'I was betrayed at the wrong moment. The Fool arranged for me to be caught after I'd left the gallery with the scepter.'

'But what of the original painting? Where did you hide it?' He hesitated. 'It's still in the palace, isn't it?'

'After a fashion.'

Gaotona looked at her, still smiling.

'I burned it,' Shai said.

The smile vanished immediately. 'You lie.'

'Not this time, old man,' Shai said. 'The painting wasn't worth the risk to get it out of the gallery. I only pulled that swap to test security. I got the fake in easily; people aren't searched going in, only coming out. The scepter was my true goal. Stealing the painting was secondary. After I replaced it, I tossed the original into one of the main gallery hearths.'

'That's *horrible*,' Gaotona said. 'It was an original ShuXen, his greatest masterpiece! He's gone blind, and can no longer paint. Do you realize the cost . . .' He sputtered. 'I don't understand. Why, *why* would you do something like that?'

'It doesn't matter. No one will know what I've done. They will keep looking at the fake and be satisfied, so there's no harm done.'

'That painting was a priceless work of art!' Gaotona glared at her. 'Your swap of it was about pride and nothing else. You didn't care about selling the original. You just wanted your copy hanging in the gallery instead. You destroyed something wonderful so that you could elevate yourself!'

She shrugged. There was more to the story, but the fact was, she *had* burned the painting. She had her reasons.

'We are done for the day,' Gaotona said, red faced.

He waved a hand at her, dismissive as he stood up. 'I had begun to think . . . Bah!'

He stalked out the door.

DAY FORTY-TWO

EACH PERSON WAS a puzzle.

That was how Tao, her first trainer in Forgery, had explained it. A Forger wasn't a simple scam artist or trickster. A Forger was an artist who painted with human perception.

Any grime-covered urchin on the street could scam someone. A Forger sought loftier heights. Common scammers worked by pulling a cloth over someone's eyes, then fleeing before realization hit. A Forger had to create something so perfect, so beautiful, so *real* that their subjects never questioned.

A person was like a dense forest thicket, overgrown with a twisting mess of vines, weeds, shrubs, saplings, and flowers. No person was one single emotion; no person had only one desire. They had many, and usually those desires conflicted with one another like two rosebushes fighting for the same patch of ground.

Respect the people you lie to, Tao had taught her. Steal from them long enough, and you will begin to understand them.

Shai crafted a book as she worked, a true history of Emperor Ashravan's life. It would become a truer history than those his scribes had written to glorify him, a truer history even than the one written by his own hand. Shai slowly pieced together the puzzle, crawling into the thicket that had been Ashravan's mind.

He *had* been idealistic, as Gaotona said. She saw it now in the cautious worry of his early writings and in the way he had treated his servants. The empire was not a terrible thing. Neither was it a wonderful thing. The empire simply *was*. The people suffered its rule because they were comfortable with its little tyrannies. Corruption was inevitable. You lived with it. It was either that or accept the chaos of the unknown.

Grands were treated with extreme favoritism. Entering government service, the most lucrative and prestigious of occupations, was often more about bribes and connections than it was about skill or aptitude. In addition, some of those who best served the empire – merchants and laborers – were systematically robbed by a hundred hands in their pockets.

Everyone knew these things. Ashravan had wanted to change them. At first.

And then … Well, there hadn't been a specific *and then*. Poets would point to a single flaw in Ashravan's nature that had led him to failure, but a person was no more one flaw than they were one passion. If Shai based her Forgery on any single attribute, she would create a mockery, not a man.

But … was that the best she could hope for? Perhaps she should try for authenticity in one specific setting, making an emperor who could act properly in court, but could not fool those closest to him. Perhaps that would work well enough, like the stage props from a playhouse. Those served their purpose while the play was going, but failed serious inspection.

That was an achievable goal. Perhaps she should go to the arbiters, explain what was possible, and give them a lesser emperor – a puppet they could use at official functions, then whisk away with explanations that he was growing sickly.

She could do that.

She found that she didn't want to.

That wasn't the challenge. That was the street thief's version of a scam, intended for short-term gain. The Forger's way was to create something enduring.

Deep down, she was thrilled by the challenge. She found that she *wanted* to make Ashravan live. She wanted to try, at least.

Shai lay back on her bed, which by now she had Forged to something more comfortable, with posts and a deep comforter. She kept the curtains drawn. Her guards for the evening played a round of cards at her table.

Why do you care about making Ashravan live? Shai thought to herself. *The arbiters will kill you before you can even see if this works. Escape should be your only goal.*

And yet ... the *emperor* himself. She had chosen to steal the Moon Scepter because it was the most famous piece in the empire. She had wanted one of her works to be on display in the grand Imperial Gallery.

This task she now worked on, however ... this was something far greater. What Forger had accomplished such a feat? A Forgery, sitting on the Rose Throne *itself?*

No, she told herself, more forceful this time. *Don't be lured. Pride, Shai. Don't let the pride drive you.*

She opened her book to the back pages, where she'd hidden her escape plans in a cypher, disguised to look like a dictionary of terms and people.

That Bloodsealer had come in running the other day, as if frightened that he'd be late to reset his seal. His clothing had smelled of strong drink. He was enjoying the palace's hospitality. If she could make him come early one morning, then ensure that he got extra drunk that night . . .

The mountains of the Strikers bordered Dzhamar, where the swamps of the Bloodsealers were located. Their hatred of one another ran deep, perhaps deeper than their loyalty to the empire. Several of the Strikers in particular seemed revolted when the Bloodsealer came. Shai had begun befriending those guards. Jokes in passing. Mentions of a coincidental similarity in her background and theirs. The Strikers weren't supposed to talk to Shai, but weeks had passed without Shai doing anything more than poring through books and chatting with old arbiters. The guards were bored, and boredom made people easy to manipulate.

Shai had access to plenty of soulstone, and she would use it. However, often more elementary methods were of greater use. People always expected a Forger to use seals for everything. Grands told stories of dark witchcraft, of Forgers placing seals on a person's feet while they slept, changing their personalities. Invading them, raping their minds.

The truth was that a soulstamp was often a Forger's last resort. It was too easy to detect. *Not that I wouldn't give my right hand for my Essence Marks right now . . .*

Almost, she was tempted to try carving a new Mark to use in getting away. They'd be expecting that, however, and she would have real trouble performing the hundreds of tests she'd need to do to make one work. Testing on her own arm would be reported by the guards, and testing on Gaotona would never work.

And using an Essence Mark she hadn't tested . . . well, that could go very, very poorly. No, her plans for escape would use soulstamps, but their heart would involve more traditional methods of subterfuge.

DAY FIFTY-EIGHT

SHAI WAS READY when Frava next visited.

The woman paused in the doorway, the guards shuffling out without objection as Captain Zu took their place. 'You've been busy,' Frava noted.

Shai looked up from her research. Frava wasn't referring to her progress, but to the room. Most recently, Shai had improved the floor. It hadn't been difficult. The rock used to build the palace – the quarry, the dates, the stonemasons – all were matters of historic record.

'You like it?' Shai asked. 'The marble works well with the hearth, I think.'

Frava turned, then blinked. 'A *hearth?* Where did you ... Is this room bigger than it was?'

'The storage room next door wasn't being used,' Shai mumbled, turning back to her book. 'And the division between these two rooms was recent, constructed only a few years back. I rewrote the construction so that this room was made the larger of the two, and so that a hearth was installed.'

Frava seemed stunned. 'I wouldn't have thought ...' The woman looked back to Shai, and her face adopted its usual severe mask. 'I find it difficult to believe that you are taking your duty seriously, Forger. You are here to make an emperor, not remodel the palace.'

'Carving soulstone relaxes me,' Shai said. 'As does having a workspace that doesn't remind me of a closet. You will have your emperor's soul in time, Frava.'

The arbiter stalked through the room, inspecting the desk. 'Then you have begun the emperor's soulstone?'

'I've begun many of them,' Shai said. 'It will be a complex process. I've tested well over a hundred stamps on Gaotona—'

'*Arbiter* Gaotona.'

'—on the old man. Each is only a tiny slice of the puzzle. Once I have all of the pieces working, I'll recarve them in smaller, more delicate etchings. That will allow me to combine about a dozen test stamps into one final stamp.'

'But you said you'd tested over a hundred,' Frava said, frowning. 'You'll only use twelve of those in the end?'

Shai laughed. 'Twelve? To Forge an entire *soul?* Hardly. The final stamp, the one you will need to use on the emperor each morning, will be like ... a linchpin, or the keystone of an arch. It will be the only one that will need to be placed on his skin, but it will connect a lattice of hundreds of other stamps.'

Shai reached to the side, taking out her book of notes, including initial sketches of the final stamps. 'I'll take these and stamp them onto a metal plate, then link that to the stamp you will place on Ashravan each day. He'll need to keep the plate close at all times.'

'He'll need to carry a metal plate with him,' Frava said drily, '*and* he will need to be stamped each day? This will make it difficult for the man to live a normal life, don't you think?'

'Being emperor makes it difficult for any man to live a

normal life, I suspect. You will make it work. It's customary for the plate to be designed as a piece of adornment. A large medallion, perhaps, or an upper arm bracer with square sides. If you look at my own Essence Marks, you'll notice they were done in the same way, and that the box contains a plate for each one.' Shai hesitated. 'That said, I've never done this exact thing before; no one has. There is a chance ... and I'd say a fair one ... that over time, the emperor's brain will absorb the information. Like ... like if you traced the exact same image on a stack of papers every day for a year, at the end the layers below will contain the image as well. Perhaps after a few years of being stamped, he won't need the treatment any longer.'

'I still name it egregious.'

'Worse than being dead?' Shai asked.

Frava rested her hand on Shai's book of notes and half-finished sketches. Then she picked it up. 'I will have our scribes copy this.'

Shai stood up. 'I need it.'

'I'm sure you do,' Frava said. 'That is precisely why it should be copied, just in case.'

'Copying it will take too long.'

'I will have it back to you in a day,' Frava said lightly, stepping away. Shai reached for her, and Captain Zu stepped up, sword already half out of its sheath.

Frava turned to him. 'Now, now, Captain. That won't be needed. The Forger is protective of her work. That is good. It shows that she is invested.'

Shai and Zu locked gazes. *He wants me dead,* Shai thought. *Badly.* She'd figured him out by now. Guarding the palace was his duty, one that Shai had invaded by her theft. Zu hadn't captured her; the Imperial Fool had turned her in. Zu felt insecure because of his failure, and so he wanted to remove Shai in retribution.

Shai eventually broke his gaze. Though it galled her, she needed to take the submissive side of this interaction. 'Be careful,' she warned Frava. 'Do not let them lose even a single page.'

'I will protect this as if . . . as if the emperor's life depended on it.' Frava found her joke amusing, and she gave Shai a rare smile. 'You have considered the other matter we discussed?'

'Yes.'

'And?'

'Yes.'

Frava's smile deepened. 'We will talk again soon.'

Frava left with the book, nearly two months' worth of work. Shai knew exactly what the woman was up to. Frava wasn't going to have it copied – she was going to show it to her other Forger and see if it was far enough along for him to finish the job.

If he determined that it was, Shai would be executed, quietly, before the other arbiters could object. Zu would likely do it himself. It could all end here.

DAY FIFTY-NINE

SHAI SLEPT POORLY that night.

She was certain that her preparations had been thorough. And yet now, she had to wait as if with a noose around her neck. It made her anxious. What if she'd misread the situation?

She had made her notations in the book intentionally opaque, each of them a subtle indication of just how *enormous* this project was. The cramped writing, the numerous cross rcfcrcnccs, thc lists and lists of rcmindcrs to hcrsclf of things to do ... Each of these would work together with the thick book as a whole to indicate that her work was mind-breakingly complex.

It was a forgery. One of the most difficult types – a forgery that did not imitate a specific person or object. This was a forgery of *tone.*

Stay away, the tone of that book said. *You don't want to try to finish this. You want to let Shai continue to do the hard parts, because the work required to do it yourself would be enormous. And ... if you fail ... it will be your head on the line.*

That book was one of the most subtle forgeries she'd ever created. Each word in it was true and yet a lie at the same time. Only a master Forger might see through it, might notice how hard she was working to illustrate the danger and difficulty of the project.

How skilled was Frava's Forger?

Would Shai be dead before morning?

She didn't sleep. She wanted to and she should have. Waiting out the hours, minutes, and seconds was excruciating. The thought of lying in bed asleep when they came for her ... that was worse.

Eventually, she got up and retrieved some accounts of Ashravan's life. The guards playing cards at her table gave her a glance. One even nodded with sympathy at her red eyes and tired posture. 'Light too bright?' he asked, gesturing at the lamp.

'No,' Shai said. 'Just a thought in my brain that won't get out.'

She spent the night in bed pouring herself into Ashravan's life. Frustrated to be lacking her notes, she got out a fresh sheet and began some new ones she'd add to her book when it returned. If it did.

She felt that she finally understood why Ashravan had abandoned his youthful optimism. At least, she knew the factors that had combined to lead him down that path. Corruption was part of it, but not the main part. Again, lack of self-confidence contributed, but hadn't been the decisive factor.

No, Ashravan's downfall had been life itself. Life in the palace, life as part of an empire that clicked along like a clock. Everything worked. Oh, it didn't work as well as it might. But it *did* work.

Challenging that took effort, and effort was sometimes hard to muster. He had lived a life of leisure. Ashravan hadn't been lazy, but it didn't require laziness to be swept up in the workings of imperial bureaucracy – to tell yourself that next month you'd go and demand that your changes be made. Over time, it had become easier and easier to float along the course of the great river that was the Rose Empire.

In the end, he'd grown indulgent. He'd focused more on the beauty of his palace than on the lives of his subjects. He had allowed the arbiters to handle more and more government functions.

Shai sighed. Even that description of him was too simplistic. It neglected to mention *who* the emperor had been, and who he had become. A chronology of events didn't speak of his temper, his fondness for debate, his eye for beauty, or his habit of writing terrible, *terrible* poetry and then expecting all who served him to tell him how wonderful it was.

It also didn't speak of his arrogance, or his secret wish that he could have been something else. That was why he had gone back over his book again and again. Perhaps he had been looking for that branching point in his life where he had stepped down the wrong path.

He hadn't understood. There was rarely an obvious branching point in a person's life. People changed slowly, over time. You didn't take one step, then find yourself in a completely new location. You first took a little step off a path to avoid some rocks. For a while, you walked alongside the path, but then you wandered out a little way to step on softer soil. Then you stopped paying attention as you drifted farther and farther away. Finally, you found yourself in the wrong city, wondering why the signs on the roadway hadn't led you better.

The door to her room opened.

Shai bolted upright in her bed, nearly dropping her notes. They'd come for her.

But … no, it was *morning* already. Light trickled through the stained glass window, and the guards were standing up and stretching. The one who had opened the door was the Bloodsealer. He looked hungover again, and carried a stack of papers in his hand, as he often did.

He's early this morning, Shai thought, checking her pocket watch. *Why early today, when he's late so often?*

The Bloodsealer cut her and stamped the door without a word, causing the pain to burn in Shai's arm. He hurried out of the room, as if off to some appointment. Shai stared after him, then shook her head.

A moment later, the door opened again and Frava entered.

'Oh, you're up,' the woman said as the Strikers saluted her. Frava set Shai's book down on the table with a thump. She seemed annoyed. 'The scribes are done. Get back to work.'

Frava left in a bustle. Shai leaned back in her bed, sighing in relief. Her ruse had worked. That should earn her a few more weeks.

DAY SEVENTY

'So this symbol,' Gaotona said, pointing at one of her sketches of the greater stamps she would soon carve, 'is a time notation, indicating a moment specifically . . . seven years ago?'

'Yes,' Shai said, dusting off the end of a freshly carved soulstamp. 'You learn quickly.'

'I am undergoing surgery each day, so to speak,' Gaotona said. 'It makes me more comfortable to know the kinds of knives being used.'

'The changes aren't—'

'Aren't permanent,' he said. 'Yes, so you keep saying.' He stretched out his arm for her to stamp. 'However, it makes me wonder. One can cut the body, and it will heal – but do it over and over again in the same spot, and you *will* scar. The soul cannot be so different.'

'Except, of course, that it's *completely* different,' Shai said, stamping his arm.

He had never quite forgiven her for what she had done in burning ShuXen's masterpiece. She could see it in him, when they interacted. He was no longer just disappointed in her, he was angry at her.

Anger faded with time, and they had a functional working relationship again.

Gaotona cocked his head. 'I ... Now *that* is odd.'

'Odd in what way?' Shai asked, watching the seconds pass on her pocket watch.

'I remember encouraging *myself* to become emperor. And ... and I resent myself. For ... mother of light, is that really how he regarded me?'

The seal remained in place for fifty-seven seconds. Good enough. 'Yes,' she said as the seal faded away. 'I believe that is exactly how he regarded you.' She felt a thrill. *Finally* that seal had worked!

She was getting close now. Close to understanding the emperor, close to having the puzzle come together. Whenever she neared the end of a project – a painting, a large-scale soul Forgery, a sculpture – there came a moment in the process where she could *see* the entire work, even if it was far from finished. When that moment came, in her mind's eye, the work was complete; actually finishing it was almost a formality.

She was nearly there with this project. The emperor's soul spread out before her, with only some few corners still shadowed. She wanted to see it through; she *longed* to find out if she could make him live again. After reading so much about him, after coming to feel as if she knew him so well, she needed to finish.

Surely her escape could wait until then.

'That was it, wasn't it?' Gaotona asked. 'That was the stamp that you've tried a dozen times without success, the seal representing why he stood up to become emperor.'

'Yes,' Shai said.

'His relationship with me,' Gaotona said. 'You made his decision depend upon his relationship with me, and ... and the sense of shame he felt when speaking with me.'

'Yes.'

'And it took.'

'Yes.'

Gaotona sat back. 'Mother of lights ...' he whispered again.

Shai took the seal and put it with those that she had confirmed as workable.

Over the last few weeks, each of the other arbiters had done as Frava had, coming to Shai and offering her fantastic promises in exchange for giving them ultimate control of the emperor. Only Gaotona had never tried to bribe her. A genuine man, and one in the highest levels of imperial government no less. Remarkable. Using him was going to be far more difficult than she would have liked.

'I must say again,' she said, turning to him, 'you've impressed me. I don't think many Grands would take the time to study soulstamps. They would eschew what they considered evil without ever trying to understand it. You've changed your mind?'

'No,' Gaotona said. 'I still think that what you do is, if not evil, then certainly unholy. And yet, who am I to speak? I am depending upon you to preserve us in power by means of this art we so freely call an abomination. Our hunger for power outweighs our conscience.'

'True for the others,' Shai said, 'but that is not your personal motive.'

He raised an eyebrow at her.

'You just want Ashravan back,' Shai said. 'You refuse to accept that you've lost him. You loved him as a son – the youth that you mentored, the emperor you always believed in, even when he didn't believe in himself.'

Gaotona looked away, looking decidedly uncomfortable.

'It won't be him,' Shai said. 'Even if I succeed, it won't *truly* be him. You realize this, of course.'

He nodded.

'But then ... sometimes a clever Forgery is as good as the real thing,' Shai said. 'You are of the Heritage Faction. You surround yourself with relics that aren't truly relics, paintings that are imitations of ones long lost. I suppose having a fake relic for an emperor won't be so different. And you ... you just want to know that you've done everything you could. For him.'

'How do you do it?' Gaotona asked softly. 'I've seen how you speak with the guards, how you learn even the names of the servants. You seem to know their family lives, their passions, what they do in the evenings ... and yet you spend each day locked in this room. You haven't left it for months. How do you know these things?'

'People,' Shai said, rising to fetch another seal, 'by nature attempt to exercise power over what is around them. We build walls to shelter us from the wind, roofs to stop the rain. We tame the elements, bend nature to our wills. It makes us feel as if we're in control.

'Except in doing so, we merely replace one influence with another. Instead of the wind affecting us, it is a wall. A *man-made* wall. The fingers of man's influence are all about, touching everything. Man-made rugs, man-made food. Every single thing in the city that we touch, see, feel, *experience* comes as the result of some person's influence.

'We may feel in control, but we never truly are unless we

understand people. Controlling our environment is no longer about blocking the wind, it's about knowing why the serving lady was crying last night, or why a particular guard always loses at cards. Or why your employer hired you in the first place.'

Gaotona looked back at her as she sat, then held out a seal to him. He hesitantly proffered an arm. 'It occurs to me,' he said, 'that even in our extreme care not to do so, we have underestimated you, woman.'

'Good,' she said. 'You're paying attention.' She stamped him. 'Now tell me, why exactly do you hate fish?'

DAY SEVENTY-SIX

I NEED TO *do it,* Shai thought as the Bloodsealer cut her arm. *Today. I could go today.*

Hidden in her other sleeve, she carried a slip of paper made to imitate the ones that the Bloodsealer often brought with him on the mornings that he came early.

She'd caught sight of a bit of wax on one of them two days back. They were letters. Realization had dawned. She'd been wrong about this man all along.

'Good news?' she asked him as he inked his stamp with her blood.

The white-lipped man gave her a sneering glance.

'From home,' Shai said. 'The woman you're writing, back in Dzhamar. She sent you a letter today? Post comes in the mornings here at the palace. They knock at your door, deliver a letter ...' *And that wakes you up*, she added in her mind. *That's why you come on time those days.* 'You must miss her a lot if you can't bear to leave her letter behind in your room.'

The man lowered his arm and grabbed Shai by the front of her shirt. 'Leave her alone, witch,' he hissed. 'You ... you *leave her alone!* None of your trickery or magics!'

He was younger than she had assumed. That was a common mistake with Dzhamarians. Their white hair and skin made them seem ageless to outsiders. Shai should have known better. He was little more than a youth.

She drew her lips to a line. 'You talk about *my* trickery and magics while holding in your hands a seal inked with my blood? You're the one threatening to send skeletals to hunt me, friend. All I can do is polish the odd table.'

'Just ... just ... Ah!' The young man threw his hands up, then stamped the door.

The guards watched with nonchalant amusement and disapproval. Shai's words had been a calculated reminder that she was harmless while the Bloodsealer was the *truly* unnatural one. The guards had spent nearly three months watching her tinker about as a friendly scholar while this man drew her blood and used it for arcane horrors.

I need to drop the paper, she thought to herself, lowering her sleeve, meaning to let her forgery slip out as the guards turned away. That would put her plan into motion, her escape ...

The real Forgery isn't finished yet. The emperor's soul.

She hesitated. Foolishly, she hesitated.

The door closed.

The opportunity passed.

Feeling numb, Shai walked to her bed and sat down on its edge, the forged letter still hidden in her sleeve. Why had she hesitated? Were her instincts for self-preservation so weak?

I can wait a little longer, she told herself. *Until Ashravan's Essence Mark is done.*

She'd been saying that for days now. Weeks, really. Each day she got closer to the deadline was another chance for Frava to strike. The woman came back with other excuses to take Shai's notes and have them inspected. They were quickly approaching the point where the other Forger wouldn't have to sort through much in order to finish Shai's work.

At least, so he would think. The further she progressed, the more impossible she realized this project was. And the more she longed to make it work anyway.

She got out her book on the emperor's life and soon found herself looking back through his youthful years. The thought of him not living again, of all of her work being merely a sham intended to distract while she planned to escape … those thoughts were physically *painful.*

Nights, Shai thought at herself. *You've grown fond of him. You're starting to see him like Gaotona does!* She shouldn't feel that way. She'd never met him. Besides, he was a despicable person.

But he hadn't always been. No, in truth, he hadn't ever *truly* become despicable. He had been more complex than that. Every person was. She could understand him, she could see—

'Nights!' she said, standing up and putting the book aside. She needed to clear her mind.

When Gaotona came to the room six hours later, Shai was just pressing a seal against the far wall. The elderly man opened the door and stepped in, then froze as the wall flooded with color.

Vine patterns spiraled out from Shai's stamp like sprays of paint. Green, scarlet, amber. The painting grew like something alive, leaves springing from branches, bunches of fruit exploding in succulent bursts. Thicker and thicker the pattern grew, golden trim breaking out of nothing and running like streams, rimming leaves, reflecting light.

The mural deepened, every inch imbued with an illusion of movement. Curling vines, unexpected thorns peeking from behind branches. Gaotona breathed out in awe and stepped up beside Shai. Behind, Zu stepped in, and the other two guards left and closed the door.

Gaotona reached out and felt the wall, but of course the paint was dry. So far as the wall knew, it had been painted like this years ago. Gaotona knelt down, looking at the two seals Shai put at the base of the painting. Only the third one, stamped above, had set off the transformation; the early seals were notes on how the image was to be created. Guidelines, a revision of history, instructions.

'How?' Gaotona asked.

'One of the Strikers guarded Atsuko of Jindo during his visit to the Rose Palace,' Shai said.' Atsuko caught a sickness, and was stuck in his bedroom for three weeks. That was just one floor up.'

'Your Forgery puts him in this room instead?'

'Yes. That was before the water damage that seeped through the ceiling last year, so it's plausible he'd have been placed here. The wall remembers Atsuko spending days too weak to leave, but having the strength for painting. A little each day, a growing pattern of vines, leaves, and berries. To pass the time.'

'This shouldn't be taking,' Gaotona said. 'This Forgery is tenuous. You've changed too much.'

'No,' Shai said. 'It's on the line ... that line where the greatest beauty is found.' She put the seal away. She barely remembered the last six hours. She had been caught up in the frenzy of creation.

'Still ...' Gaotona said.

'It will take,' Shai said. 'If you were the wall, what would you rather be? Dreary and dull, or alive with paint?'

'Walls can't think!'

'That doesn't stop them from caring.'

Gaotona shook his head, muttering about superstition. 'How long?'

'To create this soulstamp? I've been etching it here and there for the last month or so. It was the last thing I wanted to do for the room.'

'The artist was Jindoeese,' he said. 'Perhaps, because you are from the same people, it ... But no! That's thinking like your superstition.' Gaotona shook his head, trying to figure out why that painting would have taken, though it had always been obvious to Shai that this one would work.

'The Jindoeese and my people are *not* the same, by the way,' Shai said testily. 'We may have been related long ago, but we are completely different from them now.' Grands. Just because people had similar features, grands assumed they were practically identical.

Gaotona looked across her chamber and its fine furniture that had been carved and polished. Its marble floor with silver inlay, the crackling hearth and small chandelier. A fine rug – it had once been a bed quilt with holes in it – covered the floor. The stained glass window sparkled on the right wall, lighting the beautiful mural.

The only thing that retained its original form was the door, thick but unremarkable. She couldn't Forge that, not with that Bloodseal set into it.

'You realize that you now have the finest chamber in the palace,' Gaotona said.

'I doubt that,' Shai said with a sniff. 'Surely the emperor's are the nicest.'

'The largest, yes. Not the nicest.' He knelt beside the

painting, looking at her seals at the bottom. 'You included detailed explanations of how this was painted.'

'To create a realistic Forgery,' Shai said, 'you must have the technical skill you are imitating, at least to an extent.'

'So you could have painted this wall yourself.'

'I don't have the paints.'

'But you *could* have. You could have demanded paints. I'd have given them to you. Instead, you created a Forgery.'

'It's what I am,' Shai said, growing annoyed at him again.

'It's what you choose to be. If a wall can desire to be a mural, Wan ShaiLu, then *you* could desire to become a great painter.'

She slapped her stamp down on the table, then took a few deep breaths.

'You have a temper,' Gaotona said. 'Like him. Actually, I know exactly how that feels now, because you have given it to me on several occasions. I wonder if this … thing you do could be a tool for helping to bring awareness to people. Inscribe your emotions onto a stamp, then let others *feel* what it is to be you …'

'Sounds great,' Shai said. 'If only Forging souls weren't a horrible offense to nature.'

'If only.'

'If you can read those stamps, you've grown very good indeed,' Shai said, pointedly changing the topic. 'Almost I think you've been cheating.'

'Actually …'

Shai perked up, banishing her anger, now that it had passed the initial flare-up. What was this?

Gaotona sheepishly reached into the deep pocket of his robe and withdrew a wooden box. The one where she kept her treasures, the five Essence Marks. Those revisions of her soul could change her, in times of need, into someone she *could* have been.

Shai took a step forward, but when Gaotona opened the box, he revealed that the stamps weren't inside. 'I'm sorry,' he said. 'But I think giving you these now would be a little … foolish on my part. It seems that any one of them could have you free from your captivity in a moment.'

'Really only two of them could manage that,' Shai said sourly, fingers twitching. Those soulstamps represented over eight years of her life's work. She'd started the first on the day she ended her apprenticeship.

'Hm, yes,' Gaotona said. Inside the small box lay sheets of metal inscribed with the separate smaller stamps that made up the blueprints of the revisions to her soul. 'This one, I believe?' He held up one of the sheets. 'Shaizan. Translated … Shai of the Fist? This would make a warrior out of you, if you stamped yourself?'

'Yes,' Shai said. So he'd been studying her Essence Marks; that was how he'd grown so good at reading her stamps.

'I understand only one tenth of what is inscribed here, if that,' Gaotona said. 'What I find is impressive. Truly, these must have taken years to craft.'

'They are … precious to me,' Shai said, forcing herself to sit down at her desk and not fixate on the plates. If she could escape with those, she could craft a new stamp with ease. It would still take weeks, but most of her work would not be lost. But if those plates were to be destroyed …

Gaotona sat down in his customary chair, nonchalantly looking through the plates. From someone else, she would have felt an implied threat. *Look what I hold in my hands; look what I could do to you.* From Gaotona, however, that was not it. He was genuinely curious.

Or was he? As ever, she could not suppress her instincts. As good as she was, someone else could be better. Just as Uncle Won had warned. Could Gaotona have been playing her for a fool all along? She felt strongly she should trust her assessment of Gaotona. But if she was wrong, it could be a disaster.

It might be anyway, she thought. *You should have run days ago.*

'Turning yourself into a soldier I understand,' Gaotona said, setting aside the plate. 'And this one as well. A woodsman and survivalist. That one looks extremely versatile. Impressive. And here we have a scholar. But why? You are already a scholar.'

'No woman can know everything,' Shai said. 'There is only so much time for study. When I stamp myself with that Essence Mark, I can suddenly speak a dozen languages, from Fen to Mulla'dil – even a few from Sycla. I know dozens of different cultures and how to move in them. I know science, mathematics, and the major political factions of the world.'

'Ah,' Gaotona said.

Just give them to me, she thought.

'But what of this?' Gaotona said. 'A beggar? Why would you want to be emaciated, and … is this showing that most of your hair would fall out, that your skin would become scarred?'

'It changes my appearance,' Shai said. 'Drastically. That's useful.' She didn't mention that in that aspect, she knew the ways of the streets and survival in a city underworld. Her lock-picking skills weren't too shabby when not bearing that seal, but with it, she was incomparable.

With that stamp on her, she could probably manage to

climb out the tiny window – that Mark rewrote her past to give her years of experience as a contortionist – and climb the five stories down to freedom.

'I should have realized,' Gaotona said. He lifted the final plate. 'That just leaves this one, most baffling of all.'

Shai said nothing.

'Cooking,' he said. 'Farm work, sewing. Another alias, I assume. For imitating a simpler person?'

'Yes.'

Gaotona nodded, putting the sheet down.

Honesty. He must see my honesty. It cannot be faked.

'No,' Shai said, sighing.

He looked to her.

'It's . . . my way out,' she said. 'I'll never use it. It's just there, if I want to.'

'Way out?'

'If I ever use that,' Shai said, 'it will write over my years as a Forger. Everything. I will forget how to make the simplest of stamps; I will forget that I was even apprenticed as a Forger. I will become something normal.'

'And you want that?'

'No.'

A pause.

'Yes. Maybe. A part of me does.'

Honesty. It was so difficult. Sometimes it was the only way.

She dreamed about that simple life, on occasion. In that morbid way that someone standing at the edge of a cliff wonders what it would be like to just jump off. The temptation is there, even if it's ridiculous.

A normal life. No hiding, no lying. She loved what she did. She loved the thrill, the accomplishment, the wonder.

But sometimes … trapped in a prison cell or running for her life … sometimes she dreamed of something else.

'Your aunt and uncle?' he asked. 'Uncle Won, Aunt Sol, they are parts of this revision. I've read it in here.'

'They're fake,' Shai whispered.

'But you quote them all the time.'

She squeezed her eyes shut.

'I suspect,' Gaotona said, 'that a life full of lying makes reality and falsehood intermix. But if you were to use this stamp, surely you would not forget everything. How would you keep the sham from yourself?'

'It would be the greatest Forgery of all,' Shai said. 'One intended to fool even me. Written into that is the belief that without that stamp, applied every morning, I'll die. It includes a history of illness, of visiting a … resealer, as you call them. A healer that works in soul-stamps. From them, my false self received a remedy, one I must apply each morning. Aunt Sol and Uncle Won would send me letters; that is part of the charade to fool myself. I've written them already. Hundreds, which – before I use the Essence Mark on myself – I will pay a delivery service good money to send periodically.'

'But what if you try to visit them?' Gaotona said. 'To investigate your childhood …'

'It's all in the plate. I will be afraid of travel. There's truth to that, as I was indeed scared of leaving my village as a youth. Once that Mark is in place, I'll stay away from cities. I'll think the trip to visit my relatives is too dangerous. But it doesn't matter. I'll never use it.'

That stamp would end her. She would forget the last twenty years, back to when she was eight and had first begun inquiring about becoming a Forger.

She'd become someone else entirely. None of the other Essence Marks did that; they rewrote some of her past, but left her with a knowledge of who she truly was. Not so with the last one. That one was to be final. It terrified her.

'This is a great deal of work for something you'll never use,' Gaotona said.

'Sometimes, that is the way of life.'

Gaotona shook his head.

'I was hired to destroy the painting,' Shai blurted out.

She wasn't quite certain what drove her to say it. She needed to be honest with Gaotona – that was the only way her plan would work – but he didn't need this piece. Did he?

Gaotona looked up.

'ShuXen hired me to destroy Frava's painting,' Shai said. 'That's why I burned the masterpiece, rather than sneaking it out of the gallery.'

'ShuXen? But ... he's the original artist! Why would *he* hire you to destroy one of his works?'

'Because he hates the empire,' Shai said. 'He painted that piece for a woman he loved. Her children gave it to the empire as a gift. ShuXen is old now, blind, barely able to move. He did not want to go to his grave knowing that one of his works was serving to glorify the Rose Empire. He begged me to burn it.'

Gaotona seemed dumbfounded. He looked at her, as if trying to pierce through to her soul. Shai didn't know why he needed to bother; this conversation had already stripped her thoroughly bare.

'A master of his caliber is hard to imitate,' Shai said, 'particularly without the original to work from. If you think about it, you'll realize I needed his help to create those fakes. He gave me access to his studies and concepts; he told me how he'd gone about painting it. He coached me through the brush strokes.'

'Why not just have you return the original to him?' Gaotona asked.

'He's dying,' Shai said. 'Owning a thing is meaningless to him. That painting was done for a lover. She is gone now, so he felt the painting should be as well.'

'A priceless treasure,' Gaotona said. 'Gone because of foolish pride.'

'It was *his* work!'

'Not any longer,' Gaotona said. 'It belonged to everyone who saw it. You should not have agreed to this. Destroying a work of art like that is *never* right.' He hesitated. 'But still, I think I can understand. What you did had a nobility to it. Your goal was the Moon Scepter. Exposing yourself to destroy that painting was dangerous.'

'ShuXen tutored me in painting as a youth,' she said. 'I could not deny his request.'

Gaotona did not seem to agree, but he did seem to understand. Nights, but Shai felt exposed.

This is important to do, she told herself. *And maybe . . .*

But he did not give her the plates back. She hadn't expected him to, not now. Not until their agreement was done – an agreement she was certain she would not live to see the end of, unless she escaped.

They worked through the last group of new stamps. Each one took for at least a minute, as she'd been almost certain they would. She had the vision now, the idea of the final soul as it would be. Once she finished the sixth stamp for the day, Gaotona waited for the next.

'That's it,' Shai said.

'All for today?'

'All forever,' Shai said, tucking away the last of the stamps.

'You're done?' Gaotona asked, sitting up straight.' Almost a month early! It's—'

'I'm *not* done,' Shai said. 'Now is the most difficult part. I have to carve those several hundred stamps in tiny detail, melding them together, then create a linchpin stamp. What I've done so far is like getting all of the paints ready, creating the color and figure studies. Now I have to put it all together. The last time I did this, it took the better part of five months.'

'And you have only twenty-four days.'

'And I have only twenty-four days,' Shai said, but felt an immediate stab of guilt. She *had* to run. Soon. She couldn't wait to finish the project.

'Then I will leave you to it,' Gaotona said, standing and rolling down his sleeve.

DAY EIGHTY-FIVE

YES, SHAI THOUGHT, scrambling along the side of her bed and rifling through her stack of papers there. The table wasn't big enough. She'd pulled her sheets tight and turned the bed into a place to set all of her stacks. *Yes, his first love was from the storybook.* That was why . . . Kurshina's red hair . . . But this would be subconscious. He wouldn't know it. Embedded deeply, then.

How had she missed that? She wasn't nearly as close to being done as she'd thought. There wasn't time!

Shai added what she'd discovered to the seal she was working on, one that combined all of the various parts of Ashravan's romantic inclinations and experiences. She included it all: the embarrassing, the shameful, the glorious. Everything she'd been able to discover, and then a little bit more, calculated risks to fill out the soul. A flirtatious encounter with a woman whose name Ashravan could not recall. Idle fancies. A near affair with a woman now dead.

This was the most difficult part of the soul for Shai to imitate, for it was the most private. Little an emperor did was ever truly secret, but Ashravan had not always been emperor.

She had to extrapolate, lest she leave the soul bare, without passion.

So private, so *powerful*. She felt closest to Ashravan as she teased out these details. Not as a voyeur; by this point, she was a part of him.

She kept two books now. The formal notes of her process said she was horribly behind; that book left out details. The other book was her true one, disguised as useless piles of notes, random and haphazard.

She really was behind, but not so far as her official documentation showed. Hopefully, that subterfuge would earn her a few extra days before Frava struck.

As Shai searched for a specific note, she ran across one of her lists for escape plans. She hesitated. *First, deal with the seal on the door*, the note read in cypher. *Second, silence the guards. Third, recover your Essence Marks, if possible. Fourth, escape the palace. Fifth, escape the city.*

She'd written further notes for the execution of each step. She wasn't ignoring the escape, not completely. She had good plans.

Her frantic attempt to finish the soul, however, drew most of her attention. *One more week*, she told herself.

If I take one more week, I will finish five days before the deadline. Then I can run.

DAY NINETY-SEVEN

'HEY,' HURLI SAID, bending down. 'What's this?'

Hurli was a brawny Striker who acted dumber than he was. It let him win at cards. He had two children – girls, both under the age of five – but was seeing one of the women guards on the side. Hurli secretly wished he could have been a carpenter like his father. He also would have been horrified if he'd realized how much Shai knew about him.

He held up the sheet of paper he'd found on the ground. The Bloodsealer had just left. It was the morning of the ninety-sixth day of Shai's captivity in the room, and she'd decided to put the plan into motion. She *had* to get out.

The emperor's seal was not yet finished. *Almost.* One more night's work, and she'd have it. Her plan required one more night of waiting anyway.

'Weedfingers must have dropped it,' Yil said, walking over. She was the other guard in the room this morning.

'What is it?' Shai asked from the desk.

'Letter,' Hurli said with a grunt.

Both guards fell silent as they read. Palace Strikers were all literate. It was required of any imperial civil servant of at least the second reed.

Shai sat quietly, tense, sipping a cup of lemon tea and

forcing herself to breathe calmly. She made herself relax even though relaxing was the last thing she wanted to do. Shai knew the letter's contents by heart. She'd written it, after all, then had dropped it covertly behind the Bloodsealer as he'd rushed out moments ago.

Brother, the letter read. *I have almost completed my task here, and the wealth I have earned will rival even that of Azalec after his work in the Southern Provinces. The captive I secure is hardly worth the effort, but who am I to question the reasoning of people paying me far too much money?*

I will return to you shortly. I am proud to say that my other mission here has been a success. I have identified several capable warriors, and have gathered sufficient samples from them. Hair, fingernails, and a few personal effects that will not be missed. I feel confident that we will have our personal guards very soon.

It went on, the writing covering both the front and the back, so that it didn't look suspicious. Shai had padded it with a lot of talk about the palace, including things that others would assume that Shai didn't know but that the Bloodsealer would.

Shai worried that the letter was too overt. Would the guards find it to be an obvious forgery?

'That KuNuKam,' Yil whispered, using a native word of theirs. It roughly translated as a man who had an anus for a mouth. 'That imperial KuNuKam!'

Apparently, they believed it really was from him. Subtlety could be lost on soldiers.

'Can I see it?' Shai asked.

Hurli held it out to her. 'Is he saying what I think?' the guard asked. 'He's been ... *gathering* things from us?'

'It might not mean the Strikers,' Shai said after reading the letter. 'He doesn't say.'

'Why would he want hair?' Yil asked. 'And fingernails?'

'They can do things with pieces of you,' Hurli said, then cursed again. 'You see what he does each day on the door with Shai's blood.'

'I don't know if he could do much with hair or fingernails,' Shai said skeptically. 'This is just bravado. Blood needs to be fresh, not more than a day old, for it to work in his stamps. He's bragging to his brother.'

'He shouldn't be doing things like that,' Hurli said.

'I wouldn't worry about it,' Shai said.

The other two shared looks. In a few minutes, the guard change occurred. Hurli and Yil left, muttering to one another, the letter shoved in Hurli's pocket. They weren't likely to hurt the Bloodsealer badly. Threaten him, yes.

The Bloodsealer was known to frequent teahouses in the area each evening. Almost she felt sorry for the man. She had deduced that when he got news from home, he was quick and punctual to her door. He sometimes looked excited. When he didn't get news, he drank. This morning, he had looked sad. No news in a while, then.

What happened to him tonight would not make his day any better. Yes, Shai almost felt sorry for him, but then she remembered the seal on the door and the bandage she'd tied on her arm after he'd drawn blood today.

As soon as the guard change was accomplished, Shai took a deep breath, then dug back into her work.

Tonight. Tonight, she would finish.

DAY NINETY-EIGHT

SHAI KNELT ON the floor amid a pattern of scattered pages, each filled with cramped script or drawings of seals. Behind her, morning opened her eyes, and sunlight seeped through the stained glass window, spraying the room with crimson, blue, violet.

A single soulstamp, carved from polished stone, rested facedown on a metal plate sitting before her. Soulstone, as a rock, looked not unlike soapstone or another fine-grained stone, but with bits of red mixed in. As if drops of blood had stained it.

Shai blinked tired eyes. Was she really going to try to escape? She'd had ... what? Four hours of sleep in the last three days combined?

Surely escape could wait. Surely she could rest, just for today.

Rest, she thought numbly, *and I will not wake.*

She remained in place, kneeling. That stamp seemed the most beautiful thing she had ever seen.

Her ancestors had worshipped rocks that fell from the sky at night. The souls of broken gods, those chunks had been called. Master craftsmen would carve them to bring out the shape. Once, Shai had found that foolish. Why worship something you yourself created?

Kneeling before her masterpiece, she understood. She felt as if she'd bled everything into that stamp. She had pressed two years' worth of effort into three months, then had topped it off with a night of desperate, frantic carving. During that night, she'd made changes to her notes, to the soul itself. Drastic changes. She still didn't know if they had been provoked by her final, awesome vision of the project as a whole ... or if those changes had instead been faulty ideas born of fatigue and delusion.

She wouldn't know until the stamp was used.

'Is it ... is it done?' asked one of her guards. The two of them had moved to the far edge of the room, to sit beside the hearth and give her room on the floor. She vaguely remembered shoving aside the furniture. She'd spent part of the time pulling stacks of paper out from their placc bcncath thc bcd, then crawling under to fetch others.

Was it done?

Shai nodded.

'What is it?' the guard asked.

Nights, she thought. *That's right. They don't even know.* The common guards left each day during her conversations with Gaotona.

The poor Strikers would probably find themselves assigned to some remote outpost of the empire for the rest of their lives, guarding the passes leading down to the distant Teoish Peninsula or the like. They would be quietly brushed under the rug to keep them from revealing, even accidentally, anything of what had happened here.

'Ask Gaotona if you want to know,' Shai said softly. 'I am not allowed to say.'

Shai reverently picked up the seal, then placed both it and

its plate inside a box she had prepared. The stamp nestled in red velvet, the plate – shaped like a large, thin medallion – in an indentation underneath the lid. She closed the lid, then pulled over a second, slightly larger box. Inside lay five seals, carved and prepared for her upcoming escape. If she managed it. Two of them she'd already used.

If she could just sleep for a few hours. Just a few . . .

No. I can't use the bed anyway.

Curling up on the floor sounded wonderful, however.

The door began to open. Shai felt a sudden, striking moment of panic. Was it the Bloodsealer? He was supposed to be stuck in bed, having drunk himself to a stupor after being roughed up by the Strikers!

For a moment, she felt a strange guilty sense of relief. If the Bloodsealer had come, she wouldn't have a chance to escape today. She could sleep. Had Hurli and Yil not thrashed him? Shai had been sure that she'd read them correctly, and . . .

. . . and, in her fatigue, she realized she'd been jumping to conclusions. The door opened all the way, and someone did enter, but it was not the Bloodsealer.

It was Captain Zu.

'Out,' he barked at the two guards.

They jumped into motion.

'In fact,' Zu said, 'you're relieved for the day. I'll watch until the shift changes.'

The two saluted and left. Shai felt like a wounded elk being abandoned by the herd. The door clicked closed, and Zu slowly, deliberately, turned to look at her.

'The stamp isn't ready yet,' Shai lied. 'So you can—'

'It doesn't need to be ready,' Zu said, smiling a wide, thick-lipped smile. 'I believe I promised you something three months ago, thief. We have an … unsettled debt.'

The room was dim, her lamp having burned low and morning only just breaking. Shai backed away from him, quickly revising her plans. This *wasn't* how it was supposed to go. She couldn't fight Zu.

Her mouth kept moving, keeping him distracted but also playing a part she devised for herself on the fly. 'When Frava finds out you came here,' Shai said, 'she will be furious.'

Zu drew his sword.

'Nights!' Shai said, backing up to her bed. 'Zu, you don't need to do this. You *can't* do this. I have work that needs to be done!'

'Another will complete your work,' Zu said, leering. 'Frava has another Forger. You think you're so clever. You probably have some wonderful escape planned for tomorrow. This time, we're striking first. You didn't anticipate *this*, did you, liar? I'm going to enjoy killing you. Enjoy it so much.'

He lunged with the sword, its tip catching her blouse and ripping a line through it at her side. Shai jumped away, shouting for help. She was still playing the part, but it did not require acting. Her heart thumped, panic rising, as she rounded the bed in a scramble, putting it between herself and Zu.

He smiled broadly, then jumped for her, leaping onto the bed.

It promptly collapsed. During the night, while crawling under the bed to get her notes, she had Forged the wood of the frame to have deep flaws, attacked by insects, making it fragile. She'd cut the mattress underneath in wide slashes.

Zu barely had time to shout as the bed broke completely away, crashing into the pit she'd opened in the floor below. The water damage to her room – the mildew she'd smelled when first entering – had been key. By reports, the wooden beams above would have rotted and the ceiling would have fallen in if they hadn't located the leak as quickly as they had. A simple Forgery, very plausible, made it so that the floor *had* fallen in.

Zu crashed into the empty storage room one story down. Shai stood puffing, then peered into the hole. The man lay among the broken remnants of the bed. Some of that had been stuffing and cushioning. He would probably live – she'd been intending this trap for one of the regular guards, of whom she was fond.

Not exactly how I planned it, she thought, *but workable.*

Shai rushed to the table and gathered her things. The box of stamps, the emperor's soul, some extra soulstone and ink. And the two books explaining the stamps she had created in deep complexity – the official one, and the true one.

She tossed the official one into the hearth as she passed. Then she stopped in front of the door, counting heartbeats.

She agonized, watching the Bloodsealer's mark as it pulsed. Finally, after a few tormenting minutes, the seal on the door flashed one last time ... then faded. The Bloodsealer had not returned in time to renew it.

Freedom.

Shai burst out into the hallway, abandoning her home of the last three months, a room now trimmed in gold and silver. The hallway outside had been so near, yet it felt like another country entirely. She pressed the third of her prepared stamps against her buttoned blouse, changing it to match that of the palace servants, with official insignia embroidered on the left breast.

She had little time to make her next move. Soon, either the

Bloodsealer would make his way to her room, Zu would wake from his fall, or the guards would arrive for the shift change. Shai wanted to run down the hallway, breaking for the palace stables.

She did not. Running implied one of two things – guilt or an important task. Either would be memorable. Instead, she kept her gait to a swift walk and adopted the expression of one who knew what she was doing, and so should not be interrupted.

She soon entered the better-used sections of the enormous palace. No one stopped her. At a certain carpeted intersection, she stopped herself.

To the right, down a long hallway, lay the entrance to the emperor's chambers. The seal she carried in her right hand, boxed and cushioned, seemed to leap in her fingers. Why hadn't she left it in the room for Gaotona to discover? The arbiters would hunt her less assiduously if they had the seal.

She could just leave it here, in this hallway lined with portraits of ancient rulers and cluttered with Forged urns from ancient eras.

No. She had brought it with her for a reason. She'd prepared tools to get into the emperor's chambers. She'd known all along this was what she would do.

If she left now, she'd never *truly* know if the seal worked. That would be like building a house, then never stepping inside. Like forging a sword, and never giving it a swing. Like crafting a masterpiece of art, then locking it away to never be seen again.

Shai started down the long hallway.

As soon as no one was directly in sight, she turned over one of those horrid urns and broke the seal on the bottom. It transformed back into a blank clay version of itself.

She'd had plenty of time to find out exactly where these urns were crafted and by whom. The fourth of her prepared stamps transformed the urn into a replica of an ornate golden chamber pot. Shai strode down the hallway to the emperor's quarters, then nodded to the guards, chamber pot under her arm.

'I don't recognize you,' one guard said. She didn't recognize him either, with that scarred face and squinty look. As she'd expected. The guards set to watching her had been kept separate from the others so they couldn't talk about their duties.

'Oh,' Shai said, fumbling, looking abashed. 'I am sorry, greater one. I was only assigned this task this morning.' She blushed, fishing out of her pocket a small square of thick paper, marked with Gaotona's seal and signature. She had forged both the old-fashioned way. Very convenient, how he'd let her tell him how to maintain security on the emperor's rooms.

She got through without any further difficulty. The next three rooms of the emperor's expansive chambers were empty. Beyond them was a locked door. She had to Forge the wood of that door into some that had been damaged by insects – using the same stamp she'd used on her bed – to get through. It didn't take for long, but a few seconds was enough for her to kick the door open.

Inside, she found the emperor's bedroom. It was the same place she'd been led on that first day when she'd been offered this chance. The room was empty save for him, lying in that bed. He was awake, but stared sightlessly at the ceiling.

The room was still. Quiet. It smelled … too clean. Too white. Like a blank canvas.

Shai walked up to the side of the bed. Ashravan didn't look at her. His eyes didn't move. She rested fingers on his shoulder. He had a handsome face, though he was some fifteen years her senior. That was not much for a Grand; they lived longer than most.

His was a strong face, despite his long time abed. Golden hair, a firm chin, a nose that was prominent. So different in features from Shai's people.

'I know your soul,' Shai said softly. 'I know it better than you ever did.'

No alarm yet. Shai continued to expect one any moment, but she knelt down beside the bed anyway. 'I wish that I could know you. Not your soul, but *you*. I've read about you; I've seen into your heart. I've rebuilt your soul, as best I could. But that isn't the same. It isn't knowing someone, is it? That's knowing *about* someone.'

Was that a cry outside, from a distant part of the palace?

'I don't ask much of you,' she said softly. 'Just that you live. Just that you *be*. I've done what I can. Let it be enough.'

She took a deep breath, then opened the box and took out his Essence Mark. She inked it, then pulled up his shirt, exposing the upper arm.

Shai hesitated, then pressed the stamp down. It hit flesh, and stayed frozen for a moment, as stamps always did. The skin and muscle didn't give way until a second later, when the stamp *sank* a fraction of an inch.

She twisted the stamp, locking it in, and pulled it back. The bright red seal glowed faintly.

Ashravan blinked.

Shai rose and stepped back as he sat up and looked around. Silently, she counted.

'My rooms,' Ashravan said. 'What happened? There was an attack. I was … I was wounded. Oh, mother of lights. Kurshina. She's dead.'

His face became a mask of grief, but he covered it a second later. He was emperor. He might have a temper, but so long as he was not enraged, he was good at covering what he felt. He turned to her, and living eyes – eyes that *saw* – focused on her. 'Who are you?'

The question twisted her insides, for all the fact that she'd expected it.

'I'm a kind of surgeon,' Shai said. 'You were wounded badly. I have healed you. However, what I used to do so is considered … unsavory by some parts of your culture.'

'You're a resealer,' he said. 'A … a Forger?'

'In a way,' Shai said. He would believe that because he wanted to. 'This was a difficult type of resealing. You will have to be stamped each day, and you must keep that metal plate – the one shaped like a disc in that box – with you at all times. Without these, you die, Ashravan.'

'Give it to me,' he said, holding his hand out for the stamp.

She hesitated. She wasn't certain why.

'Give it to me,' he said, more forceful.

She placed the stamp in his hand.

'Don't tell anyone what has happened here,' she said to him. 'Neither guards nor servants. Only your arbiters know of what I have done.'

The cries outside sounded louder. Ashravan looked toward them. 'If no one is to know,' he said, 'you must go. Leave this place and do not return.' He looked down at the seal. 'I should probably have you killed for knowing my secret.'

That was the selfishness he'd learned during his years in the palace. Yes, she'd gotten that right.

'But you won't,' she said.

'I won't.'

And there was the mercy, buried deeply.

'Go before I change my mind,' he said.

She took one step toward the doorway, then checked her pocket watch – well over a minute. The stamp had taken, at least for the short term. She turned and looked at him.

'What are you waiting for?' he demanded.

'I just wanted one more glimpse,' she said.

He frowned.

The shouts grew even louder.

'Go,' he said. 'Please.' He seemed to know what those shouts were about, or at least he could guess.

'Do better this time,' Shai said. 'Please.'

With that, she fled.

She had been tempted, for a time, to write into him a desire to protect her. There would have been no good reason for it, at least in his eyes, and it might have undermined the entire Forgery. Beyond that, she didn't believe that he *could* save her. Until his period of mourning was through, he could not leave his quarters or speak to anyone other than his arbiters. During that time, the arbiters ran the empire.

They practically ran it anyway. No, a hasty revision of Ashravan's soul to protect her would not have worked. Near the last door out, Shai picked up her fake chamber pot. She hefted it, then stumbled through the doors. She gasped audibly at the distant cries.

'Is that about *me*?' Shai cried. 'Nights! I didn't mean it! I know I wasn't supposed to see him. I know he's in seclusion, but I opened the wrong door!'

The guards stared at her, then one relaxed. 'It isn't you. Find your quarters and stay there.'

Shai bobbed a bow and hastened away. Most of the guards didn't know her, and so—

She felt a sharp pain at her side. She gasped. That pain felt like it did each morning, when the Bloodsealer stamped the door.

Panicked, Shai felt at her side. The cut in her blouse – where Zu had slashed her with his sword – had gone all the way through her dark undershirt! When her fingers came back, they had a couple of drops of blood on them. Just a nick, nothing dangerous. In the scramble, she hadn't even noticed she'd been cut.

But the tip of Zu's sword ... it had her blood on it. Fresh blood. The Bloodsealer had found that and had begun the hunt. That pain meant he was locating her, was attuning his pets to her.

Shai tossed the urn aside and started running.

Staying hidden was no longer a consideration. Remaining unremarkable was pointless. If the Bloodsealer's skeletals reached her, she'd die. That was it. She had to reach a horse soon, then stay ahead of the skeletals for twenty-four hours, until her blood grew stale.

Shai dashed through the hallways. Servants began pointing, others screamed. She almost bowled over a southern ambassador in red priest's armor.

Shai cursed, bolting around the man. The palace exits would be locked down by now. She *knew* that. She'd studied the security. Getting out would be nearly impossible.

Always have a backup, Uncle Won said.

She always did.

Shai stopped in the hallway, and determined – as she should have earlier – that running for the exits was pointless. She was in a near panic, with the Bloodsealer on her trail, but she *had* to think clearly.

Backup plan. Hers was a desperate one, but it was all she had. She started running again, skidding around a corner, doubling back the way she'd just come.

Nights, let me have guessed right about him, she thought. *If he's secretly a master charlatan beyond my skill, I am doomed. Oh, Unknown God, please. This time, let me be right.*

Heart racing, fatigue forgotten in the moment, she eventually skidded to a stop in the hallway leading to the emperor's rooms.

There she waited. The guards inspected her, frowning, but held their posts at the end of the hallway as they'd been trained. They called to her. It was hard to keep from moving. That Bloodsealer was getting closer and closer with his horrible pets . . .

'Why are you here?' a voice said.

Shai turned as Gaotona stepped into the hallway. He'd come for the emperor first. The others would search for Shai, but Gaotona would come for the emperor, to be certain he was safe.

Shai stepped up to him, anxious. *This*, she thought, *is probably my worst idea ever for a backup plan.*

'It worked,' she said softly.

'You tried the stamp?' Gaotona said, taking her arm and glancing at the guards, then pulling her aside well out of earshot. 'Of all the hasty, insane, foolish—'

'It *worked*, Gaotona,' Shai said.

'Why did you come to him? Why not run while you had the chance?'

'I had to know. I *had* to.'

He looked at her, meeting her eyes. Seeing through them, into her soul, as he always did. Nights, but he would have made a wonderful Forger.

'The Bloodsealer has your trail,' Gaotona said. 'He has summoned those ... *things* to catch you.'

'I know.'

Gaotona hesitated for only a moment, then brought out a wooden box from his voluminous pockets. Shai's heart leaped.

He handed it toward her, and she took it with one hand, but he did not let go. 'You knew I'd come here,' Gaotona said. 'You knew I'd have these, and that I'd give them to you. I've been played for a fool.'

Shai said nothing.

'How did you do it?' he asked. 'I thought I watched you carefully. I was *certain* I had not been manipulated. And yet I ran here, half knowing I'd find you. Knowing you'd need these. I *still* didn't realize until this very moment that you'd probably planned all of this.'

'I did manipulate you, Gaotona,' she admitted. 'But I had to do it in the most difficult way possible.'

'Which was?'

'By being genuine,' she replied.

'You can't manipulate people by being genuine.'

'You can't?' Shai asked. 'Is that not how you've made your entire career? Speaking honestly, teaching people what to expect of you, then expecting them to be honest to you in return?'

'It's not the same thing.'

'No,' she said. 'It's not. But it was the best I could manage. Everything I've said to you is true, Gaotona. The painting I destroyed, the secrets about my life and desires ... Being genuine. It was the only way to get you on my side.'

'I'm not on your side.' He paused. 'But I don't want you killed either, girl. Particularly not by those *things*. Take these. Days! Take them and go, before I change my mind.'

'Thank you,' she whispered, pulling the box to her breast. She fished in her skirt pocket and brought out a small, thick book. 'Keep this safe,' she said. 'Show it to no one.'

He took it hesitantly. 'What is it?'

'The truth,' she said, then leaned in and kissed him on the cheek. 'If I escape, I will change my final Essence Mark. The one I never intend to use ... I will add to it, and to my memories, a kindly grandfather who saved my life. A man of wisdom and compassion whom I respected very much.'

'Go, fool girl,' he said. He actually had a tear in his eye. If she hadn't been on the very edge of panic, she'd have felt proud of that. And ashamed of her pride. That was how she was.

'Ashravan lives,' she said. 'When you think of me, remember that. It *worked*. Nights, it *worked!*'

She left him, dashing down the corridor.

GAOTONA LISTENED TO the girl go, but did not turn to watch her flee. He stared at that door to the emperor's chambers. Two confused guards, and a passage into ... what?

The future of the Rose Empire.

We will be led by someone not truly alive, Gaotona thought. *The fruits of our foul labors.*

He took a deep breath, then walked past the guards and pushed open the doors to go and look upon the thing he had wrought.

Just . . . please, let it not be a monster.

SHAI STRODE DOWN the palace hallway, holding the box of seals. She ripped off her buttoned blouse – revealing the tight, black cotton shirt she wore underneath – and tucked it into her pocket. She left on her skirt and the leggings beneath. It wasn't so different from the clothing she'd trained in.

Servants scattered around her. They knew, just from her posture, to get out of the way. Suddenly, Shai felt more confident than she had in years.

She had her soul back. All of it.

She took out one of her Essence Marks as she walked. She inked it with bold strikes and returned the box of seals to her skirt pocket. Then, she slammed the seal against her right bicep and locked it into place, rewriting her history, her memories, her life experience.

In that fraction of a moment, she remembered both histories. She remembered two years spent locked away, planning, creating the Essence Mark. She remembered a lifetime of being a Forger.

At the same time, she remembered spending the last fifteen years among the Teullu people. They had adopted her and trained her in their martial arts.

Two places at once, two timelines at once.

Then the former faded, and she became Shaizan, the name the Teullu had given her. Her body became leaner, harder. The body of a warrior. She slipped off her spectacles. Her eyes had been healed long ago, and she didn't need those any longer.

Gaining access to the Teullu training had been difficult; they did not like outsiders. She'd nearly been killed by them a dozen different times during her year training. But she had succeeded.

She lost all knowledge of how to create stamps, all sense of scholarly inclination. She was still herself, and she remembered her immediate past – being captured, forced to sit in that cell. She retained knowledge – logically – of what she'd just done with the stamp to her arm, and knew that the life she now remembered was fake.

But she didn't *feel* that it was. As that seal burned on her arm, she became the version of herself that would have existed if she'd been adopted by a harsh warrior culture and lived among them for well over a decade.

She kicked off her shoes. Her hair shortened; a scar stretched from her nose down around her right cheek. She walked like a warrior, prowling instead of striding.

She reached the servants' section of the palace just before the stables, the Imperial Gallery to her left.

A door opened in front of her. Zu, tall and wide-lipped, pushed through. He had a gash on his forehead – blood seeped through the bandage there – and his clothing had been torn by his fall.

He had a tempest in his eyes. He sneered as he saw her. 'You've done it now. The Bloodsealer led us right to you. I'm going to enjoy—'

He cut off as Shaizan stepped forward in a blur and smacked the heel of her hand against his wrist, breaking it, knocking the sword from his fingers. She snapped her hand upward, chopping him in the throat. Then she curled her fingers into a fist and placed a tight, short, full-knuckled punch into his chest. Six ribs shattered.

Zu stumbled backward, gasping, eyes wide with absolute shock. His sword clanged to the ground. Shaizan stepped past him, pulling his knife from his belt and whipping it up to cut the tie on his cloak.

Zu toppled to the floor, leaving the cloak in her fingers.

Shai might have said something to him. Shaizan didn't have the patience for witticisms or gibes. A warrior kept moving, like a river. She didn't break stride as she whipped the cloak around and entered the hallway behind Zu.

He gasped for breath. He'd live, but he wouldn't hold a sword again for months.

Movement came from the end of the hallway: white-limbed creatures, too thin to be alive. Shaizan prepared herself with a wide stance, body turned to the side, facing down the hallway, knees slightly bent. It did not matter how many monstrosities the Bloodsealer had; it did not matter if she won or lost.

The challenge mattered. That was all.

There were five, in the shape of men with swords. They scrambled down the hall, bones clattering, eyeless skulls regarding her without expression beyond that of their ever-grinning, pointed teeth. Some bits of the skeletals had been replaced by wooden carvings to fix bones that had broken in battle. Each creature bore a glowing red seal on its forehead; blood was required to give them life.

Even Shaizan had never fought monsters like this before. Stabbing them would be useless. But those bits that had been replaced ... some were pieces of rib or other bones the skeletals shouldn't need to fight. So if bones were broken or removed, would the creature stop working?

It seemed her best chance. She did not consider further. Shaizan was a creature of instinct. As the things reached her, she whipped Zu's cloak around and tossed it over the head of the first one. It thrashed, striking at the cloak as she engaged the second creature.

She caught its attack on the blade of Zu's dagger, then stepped up so close she could smell its bones, and reached in just below the thing's rib cage. She grabbed the spine and yanked, pulling free a handful of vertebrae, the tip of the sternum cutting her forearm. All of the bones of each skeletal seemed to be sharpened.

It collapsed, bones clattering. She was right. With the pivotal bones removed, the thing could no longer animate. Shaizan tossed the handful of vertebrae aside.

That left four of them. From what little she knew, skeletals did not tire and were relentless. She had to be quick, or they would overwhelm her.

The three behind attacked her; Shaizan ducked away, getting around the first one as it pulled off the cloak. She grabbed its skull by the eye sockets, earning a deep cut in the arm from its sword as she did so. Her blood sprayed against the wall as she yanked the skull free; the rest of the creature's body dropped to the ground in a heap.

Keep moving. Don't slow.

If she slowed, she died.

She spun on the other three, using the skull to block one sword strike and the dagger to deflect another. She skirted around the third, and it scored her side.

She could not feel pain. She'd trained herself to ignore it in battle. That was good, because that one would have *hurt*.

She smashed the skull into the head of another skeletal,

shattering both. It dropped, and Shaizan spun between the other two. Their backhand strikes clanged against one another. Shaizan's kick sent one of them stumbling back, and she rammed her body against the other, crushing it up against the wall. The bones pushed together, and she got hold of the spine, then yanked free some of the vertebrae.

The creature's bones fell with a racket. Shaizan wavered as she righted herself. Too much blood lost. She was slowing. When had she dropped the dagger? It must have slipped from her fingers as she slammed the creature against the wall.

Focus. One left.

It charged her, a sword in each hand. She heaved herself forward – getting inside its reach before it could swing – and grabbed its forearm bones. She couldn't pull them free, not from that angle. She grunted, keeping the swords at bay. Barely. She was weakening.

It pressed closer. Shaizan growled, blood flowing freely from her arm and side.

She head-butted the thing.

That worked worse in real life than it did in stories. Shaizan's vision dimmed and she slipped to her knees, gasping. The skeletal fell before her, cracked skull rolling free from the force of the blow. Blood dripped down the side of her face. She'd split her forehead, perhaps cracked her own skull.

She fell to her side and fought for consciousness.

Slowly, the darkness retreated.

Shaizan found herself amid scattered bones in an otherwise empty hallway of stone. The only color was that of her blood.

She had won. Another challenge met. She howled a chant of her adopted family, then retrieved her dagger and cut off pieces of her blouse. She used them to bind her wounds. The blood loss was bad. Even a woman with her training would not be meeting any further challenges today. Not if they required strength.

She managed to rise and retrieve Zu's cloak – still immobilized by pain, he watched her with amazed eyes. She gathered all five skulls of the Bloodsealer's pets and tied them in the cloak.

That done, she continued down the hallway, trying to project strength – not the fatigue, dizziness, and pain she actually felt.

He will be here somewhere . . .

She yanked open a storage closet at the end of the hall and found the Bloodsealer on the floor inside, eyes glazed by the shock of having his pets destroyed in rapid succession.

Shaizan grabbed the front of his shirt and hauled him to his feet. The move almost made her pass out again. *Careful.*

The Bloodsealer whimpered.

'Go back to your swamp,' Shaizan growled softly. 'The one waiting for you doesn't care that you're in the capital, that you're making so much money, that you're doing it all for her. She wants you home. That's why her letters are worded as they are.'

Shaizan said that part for Shai, who would feel guilty if she did not.

The man looked at her, confused. 'How do you . . . *Ahhrgh!*'

He said the last part as Shaizan rammed her dagger into his leg. He collapsed as she released his shirt.

'That,' Shaizan said to him softly, leaning down, 'is so that I have some of your blood. Do not hunt me. You saw what I did to your pets. I will do worse to you. I'm taking the skulls, so you cannot send them for me again. *Go. Back. Home.*'

He nodded weakly. She left him in a heap, cowering and holding his bleeding leg. The arrival of the skeletals had driven everyone else away, including guards. Shaizan stalked toward the stables, then stopped, thinking of something. It wasn't too far off . . .

You're nearly dead from these wounds, she told herself. *Don't be a fool.*

She decided to be a fool anyway.

A short time later, Shaizan entered the stables and found only a couple of frightened stable hands there. She chose the most distinctive mount in the stables. So it was that – wearing Zu's cloak and hunkered down on his horse – Shaizan was able to gallop out of the palace gates, and not a man or woman tried to stop her.

'WAS SHE TELLING the truth, Gaotona?' Ashravan asked, regarding himself in the mirror.

Gaotona looked up from where he sat. *Was she?* he thought to himself. He could never tell with Shai.

Ashravan had insisted upon dressing himself, though he was obviously weak from his long stay in bed. Gaotona sat on a stool nearby, trying to sort through a deluge of emotions.

'Gaotona?' Ashravan asked, turning to him. 'I was wounded, as that woman said? You went to a *Forger* to heal me, rather than our trained resealers?'

'Yes, Your Majesty.'

The expressions, Gaotona thought. *How did she get those right? The way he frowns just before asking a question? The way he cocks his head when not answered immediately. The way he stands, the way he waves his fingers when he's saying something he thinks is particularly important . . .*

'A MaiPon Forger,' the emperor said, pulling on his golden coat. 'I hardly think *that* was necessary.'

'Your wounds were beyond the skill of our resealers.'

'I thought nothing was beyond them.'

'We did as well.'

The emperor regarded the red seal on his arm. His expression tightened. 'This will be a manacle, Gaotona. A weight.'

'You will suffer it.'

Ashravan turned toward him. 'I see that the near death of your liege has not made you any more respectful, old man.'

'I have been tired lately, Your Majesty.'

'You're judging me,' Ashravan said, looking back at the mirror. 'You always do. Days alight! One day I will rid myself of you. You realize that, don't you? It's only because of past service that I even consider keeping you around.'

It was uncanny. This *was* Ashravan; a Forgery so keen, so perfect, that Gaotona would never have guessed the truth if he hadn't already known. He wanted to believe that the emperor's soul had still been there, in his body, and that the seal had simply . . . uncovered it.

That would be a convenient lie to tell himself. Perhaps Gaotona would start believing it eventually. Unfortunately, he had seen the emperor's eyes before, and he knew . . . he *knew* what Shai had done.

'I will go to the other arbiters, Your Majesty,' Gaotona said, standing. 'They will wish to see you.'

'Very well. You are dismissed.'

Gaotona walked toward the door.

'Gaotona.'

He turned.

'Three months in bed,' the emperor said, regarding himself in the mirror, 'with no one allowed to see me. The resealers couldn't do anything. They can fix any normal wound. It was something to do with my mind, wasn't it?'

He wasn't supposed to figure that out, Gaotona thought. *She said she wasn't going to write it into him.*

But Ashravan had been a clever man. Beneath it all, he had *always* been clever. Shai had restored him, and she couldn't keep him from thinking.

'Yes, Your Majesty,' Gaotona said.

Ashravan grunted. 'You are fortunate your gambit worked. You could have ruined my ability to think – you could have sold my soul itself. I'm not sure if I should punish you or reward you for taking that risk.'

'I assure you, Your Majesty,' Gaotona said as he left, 'I have given myself both great rewards and great punishments during these last few months.'

He left then, letting the emperor stare at himself in the mirror and consider the implications of what had been done.

For better or worse, they had their emperor back.

Or, at least, a copy of him.

EPILOGUE: DAY ONE HUNDRED AND ONE

'AND SO I hope,' Ashravan said to the assembled arbiters of the eighty factions, 'that I have laid to rest certain pernicious rumors. Exaggerations of my illness were, obviously, wishful fancy. We have yet to discover who sent the assassins, but the murder of the empress is *not* something that will go ignored.' He looked over the arbiters. 'Nor will it go unanswered.'

Frava folded her arms, watching the copy with satisfaction, but also displeasure. *What back doors did you put into his mind, little thief?* Frava wondered. *We will find them.*

Nyen was already inspecting copies of the seals. The Forger claimed that he could retroactively decrypt them, though it would take time. Perhaps years. Still, Frava would eventually know how to control the emperor.

Destroying the notes had been clever on the girl's part. Had she guessed, somehow, that Frava wasn't really making copies? Frava shook her head and stepped up beside Gaotona, who sat in their box of the Theater of Address. She sat down beside him, speaking very softly. 'They are accepting it.'

Gaotona nodded, his eyes on the fake emperor. 'There isn't even a whisper of suspicion. What we did ... it was not only audacious, it would be presumed impossible.'

'The girl could put a knife to our throats,' Frava said. 'The proof of what we did is burned into the emperor's own body. We will need to tread carefully in coming years.'

Gaotona nodded, looking distracted. Days afire, how Frava wished she could get him removed from his station. He was the only one of the arbiters who ever took a stand against her. Just before his assassination, Ashravan had been ready to do it at her prompting.

Those meetings had been private. Shai wouldn't have known of them, so the fake would not either. Frava would have to begin the process again, unless she found a way to control this duplicate Ashravan. Both options frustrated her.

'A part of me can't believe that we actually did it,' Gaotona said softly as the fake emperor moved on to the next section of his speech, a call for unity.

Frava sniffed. 'The plan was sound all along.'

'Shai escaped.'

'She will be found.'

'I doubt it,' he said. 'We were lucky to catch her that once. Fortunately, I do not believe we have much to worry about from her.'

'She'll try to blackmail us,' Frava said. *Or she'll try to find a way to control the throne.*

'No,' Gaotona said. 'No, she is satisfied.'

'Satisfied with escaping alive?'

'Satisfied with having placed one of her creations on the throne. Once, she dared to try to fool thousands – but now she has a chance to fool millions. An entire empire. Exposing what she has done would ruin the majesty of it, in her eyes.'

Did the old fool really believe that? His naiveness often presented Frava with opportunities; she'd considered letting him keep his station simply for that reason.

The fake emperor continued his speech. Ashravan *had* liked to hear himself speak. The Forger had gotten that right.

'He's using the assassination as a means of bolstering our faction,' Gaotona said. 'You hear? The implications that we need to unify, pull together, remember our heritage of strength ... And the rumors, the ones the Glory Faction spread regarding him being killed ... by mentioning them, he weakens their faction. They gambled on him not returning, and now that he has, they seem foolish.'

'True,' Frava said. 'Did you put him up to that?'

'No,' Gaotona said. 'He refused to let me counsel him on his speech. This move, though, it feels like something the old Ashravan would have done, the Ashravan from a decade ago.'

'The copy isn't perfect, then,' Frava said. 'We'll have to remember that.'

'Yes,' Gaotona said. He held something, a small, thick book that Frava didn't recognize.

A rustling came from the back of the box, and a servant of Frava's Symbol entered, passing Arbiters Stivient and Ushnaka. The youthful messenger came to Frava's side, then leaned down.

Frava gave the girl a displeased glance. 'What can be so important that you interrupt me here?'

'I'm sorry, your grace,' the woman whispered. 'But you asked me to arrange your palace offices for your afternoon meetings.'

'Well?' Frava asked.

'Did you enter the rooms yesterday, my lady?'

'No. With the business of that rogue Bloodsealer, and the emperor's demands, and ...' Frava's frown deepened. 'What is it?'

SHAI TURNED AND looked back at the Imperial Seat. The city rolled across a group of seven large hills; a major faction house topped each of the outer six, with the palace dominating the central hill.

The horse at her side looked little like the one she'd taken from the palace. It was missing teeth and walked with its head hanging low, back bowed. Its coat looked as if it hadn't been brushed in ages, and the creature was so underfed, its ribs poked out like the slats on the back of a chair.

Shai had spent the previous days lying low, using her beggar Essence Mark to hide in the Imperial Seat's underground. With that disguise in place, and with one on the horse, she'd escaped the city with ease. She'd removed her Mark once out, however. Thinking like the beggar was ... uncomfortable.

Shai loosened the horse's saddle, then reached under it and placed a fingernail against the glowing seal there. She snapped the seal's rim with some effort, breaking the Forgery. The horse transformed immediately, back straightening, head rising, sides swelling. It danced uncertainly, head darting back and forth, tugging against the reins. Zu's warhorse was a fine animal, worth more than a small house in some parts of the empire.

Hidden among the supplies on his back was the painting that Shai had stolen, again, from Arbiter Frava's office. A forgery. Shai had never had cause to steal one of her own works before. It felt . . . amusing. She'd left the large frame cut open with a single Reo rune carved in the center on the wall behind. It did not have a very pleasant meaning.

She patted the horse on the neck. All things considered, this wasn't a bad haul. A fine horse and a painting that, though fake, was so realistic that even its owner had thought it was the original.

He's giving his speech right now, Shai thought. *I would like to have heard that.*

Her gem, her crowning work, wore the mantle of imperial power. That thrilled her, but the thrill had driven her onward. Even making him live again had not been the cause of her frantic work. No, in the end, she'd pushed herself so hard because she'd wanted to leave a few specific changes embedded within the soul. Perhaps those months of being genuine to Gaotona had changed her.

Copy an image over and over on a stack of paper, Shai thought, *and eventually the lower sheets will bear the same image, pressed down. Deep within.*

She turned, taking out the Essence Mark that would transform her into a survivalist and hunter. Frava would anticipate Shai using the roads, so she would instead make her way into the deep center of the nearby Sogdian Forest. Those depths would hide her well. In a few months, she would carefully proceed out of the province and continue on to her next task: tracking down the Imperial Fool, who had betrayed her.

For now, she wanted to be far away from walls, palaces, and courtly lies. Shai hoisted herself into the horse's saddle and bid farewell to both the Imperial Seat and the man who now ruled it.

Live well, Ashravan, she thought. *And make me proud.*

LATE THAT NIGHT, following the emperor's speech, Gaotona sat by the familiar hearth in his personal study looking at the book that Shai had given him.

And marveling.

The book was a copy of the emperor's soulstamp, in detail, with notes. Everything that Shai had done lay bare to him here.

Frava would not find an exploit to control the emperor, because there wasn't one. The emperor's soul was complete, locked tight, and all his own. That wasn't to say that he was exactly the same as he had been.

I took some liberties, as you can see, Shai's notes explained. *I wanted to replicate his soul as precisely as possible. That was the task and the challenge. I did so.*

Then I took the soul a few steps farther, strengthening some memories, weakening others. I embedded deep within Ashravan triggers that will cause him to react in a specific way to the assassination and his recovery.

This isn't changing his soul. This isn't making him a different person. It is merely nudging him toward a certain path, much as a con man on the street will strongly nudge his mark to pick a certain card. It is him. The him that could have been.

Who knows? Perhaps it is the him that would have been.

Gaotona would never have figured it out on his own, of course. His skill was faint in this area. Even if he'd been a master, he suspected he wouldn't have spotted Shai's work here. She explained in the book that her intention had been to be so subtle, so careful, that no one would be able to decipher her changes. One would have to know the emperor with extreme depth to even suspect what had happened.

With the notes, Gaotona could see it. Ashravan's near death would send him into a period of deep introspection. He would seek his journal, reading again and again the accounts of his youthful self. He would see what he had been, and would finally, truly seek to recover it.

Shai indicated the transformation would be slow. Over a period of years, Ashravan would become the man that he'd once seemed destined to be. Tiny inclinations buried deep within the interactions of his seals would nudge him toward excellence instead of indulgence. He would start thinking of his legacy, as opposed to the next feast. He would remember his people, not his dinner appointments. He would finally push the factions for the changes that he, and many before him, had noticed needed to be made.

In short, he would become a fighter. He would take that single – but so hard – step across the line from dreamer to doer. Gaotona could see it, in these pages.

He found himself weeping.

Not for the future or for the emperor. These were the tears of a man who saw before himself a *masterpiece.* True art was more than beauty; it was more than technique. It was not just imitation.

It was boldness, it was contrast, it was subtlety. In this book, Gaotona found a rare work to rival that of the greatest painters, sculptors, and poets of any era.

It was the greatest work of art he had ever witnessed.

Gaotona held that book reverently for most of the night. It was the creation of months of fevered, intense artistic transcendence – forced by external pressure, but released like a breath held until the brink of collapse. Raw, yet polished. Reckless, but calculated.

Awesome, yet unseen.

So it had to remain. If anyone discovered what Shai had done, the emperor would fall. Indeed, the very empire might shake. No one could know that Ashravan's decision to finally become a great leader had been set in motion by words etched into his soul by a blasphemer.

As morning broke, Gaotona slowly – excruciatingly – stood up beside his hearth. He clutched the book, that matchless work of art, and held it out.

Then he dropped it into the flames.

POSTSCRIPT

In writing classes, I was frequently told, 'Write what you know.' It's an adage writers often hear, and it left me confused. Write what I know? How do I do that? I'm writing fantasy. I can't know what it's like to use magic – for that matter, I can't know what it's like to be female, but I want to write from a variety of viewpoints.

As I matured in skill, I began to see what this phrase meant. Though in this genre we write about the fantastic, the stories work best when there is solid grounding in our world. Magic works best for me when it aligns with scientific principles. World building works best when it draws from sources in our world. Characters work best when they're grounded in solid human emotion and experience.

Being a writer, then, is as much about observation as it is imagination.

I try to let new experiences inspire me. I've been lucky enough in this field that I am able to travel frequently. When I visit a new country, I try to let the culture, people, and experiences there shape themselves into a story.

Recently I visited Taiwan, and was fortunate enough to visit the National Palace Museum along with my editor Sherry Wang and translator Lucie Tuan to play tour guides.

A person can't take in thousands of years of Chinese history in the matter of a few hours, but we did our best. Fortunately, I had some grounding in Asian history and lore already. (I lived for two years in Korea as an LDS missionary, and I then minored in Korean during my university days.)

Seeds of a story started to grow in my mind from this visit. What stood out most to me were the stamps. We sometimes call them 'chops' in English, but I've always called them by their Korean name of *tojang*. In Mandarin, they're called *yìn-jiàn*. These intricately carved stone stamps are used as signatures for many different Asian cultures.

During my visit to the museum, I noticed many of the familiar red stamps. Some were, of course, the stamps of the artists – but there were others. One piece of calligraphy was covered in them. Lucie and Sherry explained – ancient Chinese scholars and nobility, if they liked a work of art, would sometimes stamp it with their stamp too. One emperor in particular loved to do this, and would take beautiful sculptures or pieces of jade – centuries old – and have his stamp and perhaps some lines of his poetry carved into them.

What a fascinating mind-set. Imagine being a king, deciding that you particularly liked Michelangelo's *David*, and so having your signature carved across the chest. That's essentially what this was.

The concept was so striking, I began playing with a stamp magic in my head. Soulstamps, capable of rewriting the nature of an object's existence. I didn't want to stray too close to Soulcasting from the Stormlight world, and so instead I used the inspiration of the museum – of history – to devise a magic that allowed rewriting an object's past.

The story grew from that starting place. As the magic

aligned a great deal with a system I'd been developing for Sel, the world where *Elantris* takes place, I set the story there. (I also had based several cultures there on our-world Asian cultures, so it fit wonderfully.)

You can't always write what you know – not exactly what you know. You can, however, write what you see.

Brandon Sanderson

ACKNOWLEDGMENTS

A book like this goes out with one name on the cover, yet artwork is not created in a vacuum. What I create can only exist because of the numerous shoulders I rely upon.

I've mentioned elsewhere that this book came to be because of a trip I took to Taiwan. Many thanks go to Lucie Tuan and Sherry Wang, to whom the book is dedicated, for showing me around the city. Also, I'd like to thank Evanna Hsu and everyone else at Fantasy Foundation for making that trip such a powerful experience. Many thanks to Gray Tan (my Taiwan agent) who facilitated the trip, and to my U.S. agent Joshua Bilmes and everyone else at JABberwocky.

Jacob Weisman and Jill Roberts at Tachyon have been absolutely wonderful to work with, and I thank them for giving this work a home. Also, thank you to Marty Halpern for the copyedit and proofread.

Mary Robinette Kowal is responsible for the current structure of the novella; she helped me realize my original prologue wasn't the best for the integrity of the work. Moshe Feder went above and beyond his job description (at a different publisher) to offer me fantastic line edits, without which this book would have been much the poorer. I also got important feedback from Brian Hill, Isaac Stewart, and Karen Ahlstrom.

As always, I give loving thanks to my family, particularly my wife Emily. In addition, special thanks go out to the interpolated Peter Ahlstrom, who worked long hours on this project. (Even so far as to nudge me to get this acknowledgments page written after I'd forgotten to do so about a dozen times.)

You have my deepest gratitude, all of you.
Brandon